THE MYSTERIOUS WORLD OF
SHERLOCK HOLMES

THE MYSTERIOUS WORLD OF
SHERLOCK HOLMES

BRUCE WEXLER

CHARTWELL
BOOKS

This edition published in 2015 by
CHARTWELL BOOKS
an imprint of Book Sales
a division of Quarto Publishing Group USA Inc.
276 Fifth Avenue Suite 206
New York, New York 10001
USA

ISBN-13: 978-0-7858-3020-7

Printed in China

Contents

· · · · · · · · · · · · · · ·

CHAPTER ONE

Dr. Arthur Conan Ignatius Doyle: An Author's Life

* *

Sure there are times when one cries with acidity
"Where are the limits of human stupidity?"
Here is a critic who says as a platitude
That I am guilty because "in gratitude
Sherlock, the sleuth-hound, with motives ulterior,
Sneers at Poe's Dupin as 'Very inferior.'"
Have you not learned, my esteemed communicator,
That the created is not the creator?
As the creator I've praised to satiety
Poe's Monsieur Dupin, his skill and variety,
And have admitted that in my detective work
I owe to my model a deal of selective work.
But is it not on the verge of inanity
To put down to me my creation's crude vanity?
He, the created, would scoff and sneer,
Where I, the creator, would bow and revere.
So please grip this fact with your cerebral tentacle:
The doll and its maker are never identical.

ARTHUR CONAN DOYLE, 1912

Above: Conan Doyle lectured at Toronto's Massey Hall.

It was the evening of Monday, November 26, 1894. The house lights were dimmed in Toronto's Massey Hall and there was a palpable aura of excitement and high expectation as the speaker climbed to stand behind a high desk, drenched by a single point of light. He was certainly physically impressive, "A giant in size. He looks to be about six feet four and is not at all slim" reported the *Toronto Star*. The paper went on to be somewhat critical of the speaker's declamatory style, and imply that if he had been lecturing on any other subject "he would not have been so entertaining." Fortunately, however, the speaker's subject was one that has been found continually fascinating for over 120 years, since *A Study in Scarlet* first appeared in *Beeton's Christmas Annual* for 1887. The speaker was none other than Arthur Conan Doyle, and his subject was his own creation, possibly the most recognizable fictional character ever conceived, and the world's first consulting detective: none other than the redoubtable Sherlock Holmes.

Considering that the Toronto audience was full of Holmes aficionados, ready to hang on Conan Doyle's every word concerning the great detective, the tenor of Doyle's lecture was rather strange. He was at pains to convince his audience that, not only was Holmes "no more," but that he "would not be resurrected." According to the *Toronto Star* reporter, the author maintained that his personal literary interest was in writing "bright pictures of chivalry and deeds of daring like those in which Scott won his fame." Conan Doyle's literary canon does indeed contain many works of historical fiction, but these have substantially withered away from disregard. Conan Doyle continued his address by further distancing himself from his famous creation, whom he dismissed as his "doll." The author also maintained that, far from having any ability to solve mysterious crimes himself, Holmes was actually far from being sharp, and had only the ability to "put himself in the position of a shrewd man and imagine what the shrewd man would do."

Conan Doyle's most famous creation had actually already been sent to his demise. The *Strand* had published "The Final Problem," the last story in the second series of Holmes stories, in December 1893, and for all his readers knew, the great man had fallen at Reichenbach never to return. (In novel form, these stories were published as *The Memoirs of Sherlock Holmes*). A chance visit to the Reichenbach Falls in Switzerland had presented Conan Doyle with an irresistible idea for Holmes's demise, and he was quick to grasp it. He was already sick of writing about Holmes. The adventures of his famous detective tortured him with the constant need for plotting, devising, counter-plotting, and resolution. He wanted to exorcize himself of his wearisome creation, and had written to his mother "I am in the middle of the last Holmes story, after which the gentleman vanishes never to return! I am weary of his name." He did this even in the full knowledge of the financial implications for him and his family, "I must save my mind for better things… even if it means I must bury my pocketbook with him." Conan Doyle planned to abandon the Holmes series as early as 1891, when he confessed, "I have had such an overdose of [Holmes] that I feel towards him as I do toward pate de foie gras, of which I once ate too much, so that the name of it gives me a sickly feeling to this day." It seems that, at this point at least, author and character were in accord. As Holmes writes in a note discovered (after his cryptic disappearance) by his faithful associate Watson, "my career had in any case reached its crisis, and no possible conclusion to it could be more congenial to me than this."

Apart from reading from a variety of his own work, the balance of

Conan Doyle's lecture was largely autobiographical. He sketched his own literary career, which supposedly began when the great novelist William Thackeray took the juvenile Arthur Conan Doyle onto his lap. He subsequently wrote his first story at the age of six: an illustrated work that concentrated on men and tigers.

In fact, Conan Doyle's artistic ability was deeply ingrained in his family heritage. His grandfather was the renowned caricaturist John Doyle. Born in 1797 into an impoverished Roman Catholic family in Dublin, Ireland, John Doyle had attempted to earn a living as a portrait painter, but had been forced to immigrate to London (in 1821) in an attempt to further his career. Although he exhibited at the prestigious Royal Academy, Doyle had failed to turn this to commercial advantage and he turned to lithography instead. Cartoons were hugely popular at this time, and his work regularly appeared in the *Times* for over twenty years (identified by the monogram H. B.). Doyle was well known to his great contemporary, novelist William Thackeray, who described his cartoons as "polite points of wit, which strike one as exceedingly clever and pretty, and cause one to smile in a quiet, gentlemanly kind of way." His work was in sharp contrast to fellow cartoonists James Gillray and Thomas Rowlandson, whose pens dripped with caustic satire.

John Doyle died in 1868, but two of his sons, Richard and Charles, continued the family's artistic tradition. Richard was a cartoonist. Charles was also an accomplished artist who painted, illustrated books, and worked as a sketch artist at criminal trials. Unfortunately, whereas Richard made a good living illustrating fairy stories and Charles Dickens's Christmas books for *Punch* magazine, Charles proved to be the only Doyle who was unable to turn his undoubted talent into a steady income.

Above: A political cartoon by Conan Doyle's grandfather, John Doyle.

Opposite: Sidney Paget's famous illustration of Holmes's untimely demise at the Reichenbach Falls, engineered by Conan Doyle in 1893. The scene was inspired by the author's travels in Switzerland.

Below: The author's birthplace in Edinburgh, Scotland.

Above: Arthur Conan Doyle as a young boy with his father Charles.

Despite this, his son, Conan Doyle, always considered his father to be the most gifted artist in the family. Charles married the accomplished Mary Foley on July 31, 1855. He had met her at her widowed mother's Edinburgh boarding house, having relocated to the city from England in 1849 to take up a post in Her Majesty's office of Works. Although the marriage proved to be disastrous, as Charles fell prey to depression, drink, and epilepsy, the couple produced ten children. Seven survived to adulthood. Their second child and eldest son, Arthur, was born at the family home, 11 Picardy Place, Edinburgh, on May 22, 1859. From the very beginning, Mary was the chief cultural and emotional influence on her son's life. In particular, Mary told her son "vivid stories" that he was to remember all his life. Conan Doyle's second wife, Jean, described Mary as a "very remarkable and highly cultural woman. She had a dominant personality, wrapped up in the most charming womanly exterior."

When Arthur reached the age of nine in 1868, his more prosperous relatives decided to send him to Hodder, the preparatory school for the Jesuit College at Stonyhurst. He entered the upper school in 1870 and was to spend five years there. Located in the Ribble Valley in Lancashire, the school was part of the English public school system, and was notorious for its stern regime and harsh corporal punishment. Doyle's time at the school was largely miserable. But there were some positive outcomes. The first was lifelong correspondence with his mother, "the Ma'am," which he began while at school. The second was a lifelong interest in sports and sportsmanship. His cricketing abilities were particularly renowned. The third were some colorful characters that later appeared in his fiction: he met two Moriartys at Stonyhurst.

Arthur matriculated from Stonyhurst with honors in 1875, and spent the following year at the Jesuit school at Feldkirch in Austria. Unfortunately, this exciting time coincided with his father's dismissal from the civil service in 1876. By the time Arthur left school, his father's mental health had deteriorated so seriously that one of his first grim tasks as an adult was to co-sign papers to commit Charles Doyle. Doyle had initially been sent to Fourdoun House, a nursing home that specialized in the treatment of alcoholics. But a violent escape attempt had resulted in his committal to the Montrose Royal Lunatic Asylum. Charles was to remain institutionalized until his death in 1893.

Charles's departure ushered in a different way of living for the family. Forced to take in lodgers to make ends meet, Mary Doyle had met medical man and pathologist Dr. Bryan Charles Waller. In effect, Waller became Mary's unacknowledged partner, and in 1883, she moved to the Waller family estate in Yorkshire with one of her daughters. She was to live there, rent free, for decades. Waller also became highly influential in Conan Doyle's life, and the young man decided to abandon the Doyle family's artistic tradition to train as a doctor. He duly enrolled at Edinburgh University's prestigious Medical School with Waller's moral and financial support. Ironically, Conan Doyle met two other men who were to become famous literary figures at the University, James Barrie, and Robert Louis Stephenson. It was during his university career that Conan Doyle first saw his work in print. His first published short story, "The Mystery of Sasassa Valley," appeared in the Edinburgh magazine *Chamber's Journal* in 1879, while (in complete contrast), the *British Medical Journal* published his paper "Gelseminum as a Poison" in the same year.

Above: Conan Doyle spent five years at Stonyhurst, a traditional English public school.

Below: Edinburgh University's prestigious medical school, as it was in Victorian times when Doyle studied there.

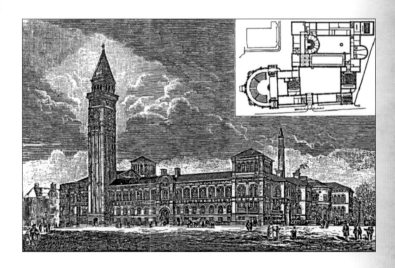

Conan Doyle's most significant university experience, however, was his 1876 meeting with Dr. Joseph Bell. Famous for his brilliant and original lectures, Bell was also Queen Victoria's personal surgeon during her frequent visits to Scotland. His intellectual approach to gathering circumstantial evidence to make astonishingly accurate medical diagnoses was inspirational. The professor applied the "trained use of observation" to assess his patients, gathering hoards of seemingly trivial information to create a meaningful picture of the whole person. Remind you of anyone? Conan Doyle became one of Bell's favored students, and during his second year at medical school, he was Bell's clerk at the Royal Infirmary's open clinic. Over a century later, the Conan Doyle/Bell relationship was immortalized in a series of books by David Pirie, which was filmed for television as *The Murder Rooms*. Conan Doyle was fully conscious of his debt to Bell's forensic detective work and wrote, "It is to you that I owe

Right: Dr. Joseph Bell lectured at the medical school and provided Conan Doyle with much of the inspiration he needed to create Holmes.

Sherlock Holmes." Mutual acquaintance Rudyard Kipling asked of Holmes, "Could this be my old friend, Dr. Joe?" But Holmes was not simply a pastiche of Bell's flamboyant personality. Doyle acknowledged that he derived aspects of the character from several other sources ("I owe to my model a deal of selective work"), including Edgar Allan Poe's detective character, Monsieur C. Auguste Dupin, together with the infamous Eugene Francois Vidocq. Vidocq was a reformed master criminal who became the first chief of the Surete in Paris. The "detective" writing style of both Charles Dickens and Wilkie Collins is also apparent in Conan Doyle's Sherlockian works. Throughout his student days, Conan Doyle read voraciously, including William Thackeray's *Esmond*, George Meredith's *Richard Feverel*, and Washington Irving's *Conquest in Granada*.

The creation of Holmes was still years ahead. In 1881, Conan Doyle graduated as a Bachelor of Medicine and Master of Surgery. In his third year at Edinburgh, the young medic had served as a ship's doctor on a whaling boat, *The Hope*. On graduation, his first job was as the medical officer on the Liverpool steamer *Mayumba*. While Doyle had hugely enjoyed his time aboard *The Hope* in the freezing Arctic, he hated the dirt and heat of Africa and became seriously ill from a tropical

Above: The statue of Sherlock Holmes erected in Edinburgh to honor Sir Arthur Conan Doyle.

Left: *The Hope* was a whaling boat on which Conan Doyle served as a medical officer. His hand-written log of the voyage has survived.

Right: Conan Doyle photographed outside Bush Villa in Southsea, England where he set up medical practice in the mid 1880s.

Below: Conan Doyle's brass nameplate from Bush Villa, which he kept as a souvenir after he became a famous writer.

fever. He resigned his place as soon as the ship re-docked in England. His next medical foray was to Plymouth (in 1882), to work as a doctor in practice with his former schoolmate, George Budd. But Conan Doyle became increasingly concerned about Budd's ethical standards, and their relationship fell apart in a few weeks, when Conan Doyle left the practice. He was in serious financial trouble, on the verge of bankruptcy. He moved to Southsea, Portsmouth to open his own practice. It was a fairly shoestring operation, as he could only afford to furnish the consulting rooms. Business was initially slow, which gave Arthur the chance to compose stories in between his rather sparse patients. A small flurry of short stories appeared, including "The Captain of the Polestar," "J. Habakuk Jephson's Statement," "The Heiress of Glenmahowley," "The Cabman's Story," and "The Man from Archangel." These were published in various magazines, including *Cornhill Magazine*, *Cassell's Saturday Journal*, and *Temple Bar*.

Conan Doyle also found time to get married during this period. He met Louise Hawkins ("Touie") in 1885 and married her in August of that year. The Ma'am highly approved of her son's choice. Touie was a home-loving woman, attractive rather than beautiful. Doyle described her as "gentle and amiable." 1885 also saw the publication of Conan's Doyle doctoral theses on the effects of syphilis, "An Essay Upon the Vasometer Changes in Tabes Dorsalis."

Ironically, Conan Doyle had met Touie through the sickness of her brother, John Hawkins. Hawkins had been a resident patient of Conan Doyle's at his Southsea villa, but had died of cerebral meningitis in 1885. Hawkins's death, and the subsequent marriage of his sister (and heir) to his doctor led to a great deal of local gossip. Worse was to follow. A poison pen letter about Hawkins's sudden death, and the rather hasty burial that Conan Doyle had arranged, was sent to the police. This almost resulted in an official enquiry into Hawkin's "suspicious death," and only the supportive intervention of Conan Doyle's medical neighbor averted police involvement. Perhaps this horribly close brush with the legal system explains Conan Doyle's interest in miscarriages of justice. Biographer Peter Costello describes Conan Doyle's shock realization of the "narrow margin of fate that protects the innocent, the minor twist of evidence that could acquit or hang an accused."

Above: Conan Doyle as young man in 1885, suitably attired in a debonair Edwardian "boater."

Now ensconced in a pleasant domestic life, Doyle continued with his literary ambitions. In March 1886, he finally hit upon the characters that

Right: Louise Hawkins, nicknamed "Touie," was a handsome, home-loving woman. She became Conan Doyle's first wife in 1885.

were to make his reputation and his fortune. At first, he entitled the novel *A Tangled Skein*, and the two main characters were called Sheridan Hope and Ormond Sacker. Sheridan Hope became Sherrinford Holmes, and the rest is history. The first ever Holmes story, "A Study in Scarlet," was published in *Beeton's Christmas Annual* for 1887. It is in this first Holmes story that the great detective and Watson meet. Conan Doyle was paid the princely sum of £25 and had to relinquish his copyright. Further Holmesian works, *The Sign of Four* (1890) and "A Scandal in Bohemia" were interspersed with two historical novels, *Micah Clarke* (1889) and *The White Company* (October 1891). The latter were in the romantic adventure style of Sir Walter Scott.

This body of literary work proved to be commercially successful and brought him into contact with other contemporary artists such as Oscar Wilde. Although the two men could not have been more different in character, they were instantly attracted to one another and became great friends. Conan Doyle described their meeting very warmly, as a "golden evening for me." It took place at London's Langham Hotel in 1889, in the company of American magazine publisher, Joseph Marshall Stoddart. Stoddart had traveled from Philadelphia to establish a British edition of his publication, *Lippincott's Monthly Magazine*. This new publication commissioned both Wilde's novel *The Picture of Dorian Gray*, and Conan Doyle's book *The Sign of Four*. The title effectively secured the place of Sherlock Holmes in world literature. Without Stoddart's involvement, the great detective may have been consigned to the slush pile of literary history.

The flourishing of Conan Doyle's literary career was not reflected in his medical work. He decided to specialize, and traveled to Vienna and Paris to study ophthalmology. In 1891, Conan Doyle returned to London to set up an ophthalmologic practice in the elegant Upper Wimpole Street (just off Harley Street). He would later maintain that not a single patient darkened his doors. Later that year, a serious attack of influenza laid

Right: A posed picture of Conan Doyle at his desk, taken after he had become a successful author.

The author himself made a very important professional decision, to write a collection of short stories around a single, detective, character. The stories were also unusual in that the observant Dr. Watson relates them in the first person. This gave Conan Doyle the opportunity to portray Holmes in a deeply personal and realistic way.

Conan Doyle seriously low and for several days, he hovered between life and death. As he began to recover, he realized that he should concentrate his efforts on the professional area in which he had found success, his writing. Having made this decision, Conan Doyle was delighted that he would "at last be my own master." He also decided to employ a literary agent, A. P. Watt, whose duty was to take over the "hateful bargaining" that so embarrassed Conan Doyle.

The author himself made a very important professional decision, to write a collection of short stories around a single, detective, character. The stories were also unusual in that the observant Dr. Watson relates them in the first person. This gave Conan Doyle the opportunity to portray Holmes in a deeply personal and realistic way. "A Scandal in Bohemia" duly appeared in July 1891. With this promising beginning, Doyle had hit upon a unique genre that was to bring him a great deal of critical and financial success. By October 1891, he was able to write to his mother that his publishers were "imploring him to continue Holmes."

Watt subsequently made a deal with the *Strand* magazine to publish the first six short stories featuring Holmes and Watson, and Doyle's characters were to be brought to life by Sidney Paget's brilliant illustrations. Paget used his handsome brother Walter as a model for the great detective. A collection of twelve of these Holmes stories, *The Adventures of Sherlock Holmes*, was published in 1892. In all, Doyle went on to compose fifty-six short stories and four complete novels featuring his most famous creation. *The Valley of Fear* was the last novel, published in 1914 and 1915. It is worth remembering that Conan Doyle did not write the Holmes stories chronologically, and later compilers have spent a great deal of time and effort trying to place them in the order of the events described.

By the time the Holmes stories began to appear, the Doyles had two children. Mary Louise Conan was born in 1889, and Alleyne Kingsley Conan in 1892. Arthur referred to Kingsley's appearance as the "chief event" of his life with Touie.

Having freed himself from his oppressive lack of success in the medical profession, Doyle soon began to feel that the Sherlock Holmes sensation tied him to producing these stories, and kept him from writing in the historical genre he preferred. It is extraordinary to think that this literary ennui followed almost immediately on the heels of Holmes's enormously successful introduction. By December 1893, Holmes and Moriarty were (apparently) already dead, having plunged over the Reichenbach Falls, locked in mortal combat. To the *Strand*, the end of the Holmes stories was a devastating blow; 20,000 readers cancelled their subscriptions, and dedicated followers of Holmes wore mourning in both Britain and America. Mary Doyle's advice to her son had been prophetic, "You may do what you deem fit, but the crowds will not take this lightheartedly." To Holmes devotees, the years of the "Great Hiatus" now began. Chronologically, in the "life" of Sherlock Holmes, this gap fell between 1891 and 1894, when the great man spectacularly reappeared in "The Adventure of the Empty House" (published in 1903). (As Conan Doyle said, he was able to revive the great man as "fortunately as no coroner had pronounced on his remains.") In Conan Doyle's life, the Sherlock-free hiatus lasted rather longer, from 1893 to 1901, when he penned *The Hound of the Baskervilles*. Holmes aficionados

Below: Doyle's ventures into other media were not always successful. The musical comedy *Jane Annie*, which he co-wrote with J.M. Barrie, was a complete flop.

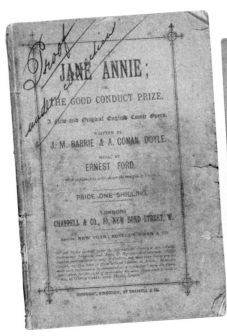

Above: Undershaw House near Hindhead, Surrey in England. Conan Doyle built the house in 1897 to provide the tubercular Touie with a healthy environment. This historic home is currently under the threat of redevelopment.

tend to end the hiatus with the short story "The Adventure of the Empty House," which features a "living" Sherlock Holmes, rather than *The Hound of the Baskervilles*, where he appears posthumously.

Not all Conan Doyle's literary endeavors were such unqualified successes. A musical comedy he co-wrote with his close friend J. M. Barrie, titled *Jane Annie,* or *The Good Conduct Prize*, was an embarrassing flop.

Disappointment over the failure of his operetta was replaced by a far more serious sorrow, when Touie was diagnosed with advanced tuberculosis. From this time on, Doyle became his wife's doctor rather than her husband, and their marital relationship began to fail. Conan Doyle became seriously depressed, and started what was to become a lifelong fascination with spiritualism, the "life beyond the veil."

For the moment, "work [was] the best antidote to sorrow" and in 1894, Conan Doyle embarked on a thirty-city lecture tour of the United States and Canada, accompanied by his younger brother Innes Doyle. This was to be the first of four trips to North America (1894, 1914, 1922, and 1923). Samuel Sidney McClure, of *McClure's Magazine*, one of Conan Doyle's American publishers, part-organized the visit. Starting in New York, it was a great success. North Americans responded well to Conan Doyle's "wholesome" personality. He was rather more ambiguous in his reciprocal feelings. In particular, he considered Canadians courageous, but dull and "unimaginative." He was, however, immediately attracted to the rugged Canadian landscape.

Conan Doyle took the American part of the tour as an opportunity to visit his literary friend Rudyard Kipling. Already rich and famous, Kipling had settled with his American wife, Caroline Belestier, in her native Vermont and they had created a beautiful estate there. Conan Doyle and Innes spent a snowy Thanksgiving at the "shingle-style" home of the Kiplings, and the two men spent their time inventing snow golf, which they played with red balls. In his autobiography, Doyle wrote that "rustics watched us from afar, wondering what on earth we were at, for golf was unknown in America at that time." In fact, this assertion was completely incorrect, but the two Englishmen must have presented an amusing spectacle, all the same.

1894 also saw the publication of Doyle's first Brigadier Gerard story ("The Medal of Brigadier Gerard") in the *Strand* magazine, the release of an autobiographical novel, *The Stark Munro Letters*, and the publication of a collection of medical short stories, *Round the Red Lamp*.

In his personal life, Touie's health continued to give cause for concern, and doctors gave her only months to live. Appalled by a vision of a nomadic life lived between the health resorts and spas of Europe, Conan Doyle was very interested to hear of the warm, dry air of Hindhead, in a small town in the leafy county of Surrey, England. The area was credited with having a micro climate of great benefit to invalids, and was known as "Little Switzerland." Conan Doyle bought a building plot in 1895 (for £1,000), and Undershaw House was completed in 1897. He collaborated with his friend, the architect Joseph Henry Ball, on the design of the thirty-six-room mansion, and they filled Undershaw with personal

Below: Manuscript and cover of the Brigadier Gerard stories. Brigadier Gerard is arguably Conan Doyle's third most successful literary character, after Holmes and Watson.

references. The entrance hall boasted a double-height stained glass window that illuminated the coats of arms of Conan Doyle's forebears, while the downstairs doors bore his monogram. His time at Undershaw, the only house he ever built for himself, was extremely productive, and many famous people visited him there, including James Barrie, Bram Stoker, and Sidney Paget. Bram Stoker was particularly charmed with Undershaw, and described how the situation of the house was "so sheltered from cold winds that the architect felt justified in having lots of windows, so that the whole place is full of light. Nevertheless, it is cozy and snug to a remarkable degree and has everywhere that sense of 'home' which is so delightful to occupant and stranger alike." The house had a profoundly beneficial effect on Touie's health, and Conan Doyle credited it with extending her life by several years. The Conan Doyle family lived at Undershaw until her death in 1906.

Despite the pressure of Touie's illness, Conan Doyle's prolific literary success continued with the publication of works in various genres, including three Captain Sharkey pirate stories, the *Round the Fire* series, and a Napoleonic novel, *Uncle Bernac*. In 1896, Conan Doyle traveled to Egypt and worked as a war correspondent, covering the fighting between the British and Dervish forces.

Conan Doyle also wrote a play that centered on his old character, Sherlock Holmes, which the famous American actor William Gillette

revised and performed for thirty-six years with great financial success. Gillette was the only actor to dramatize the character of Sherlock Holmes with the author's personal endorsement. The first of hundreds of actors to take the role, he is reputed to have given over 1,300 stage performances of Holmes between 1899 and 1932.

Personally, one of the greatest experiences of Conan Doyle's life happened the following year, on March 15, 1897. He was never to forget this date, the day he met his future wife, the twenty-four-year-old Jean Leckie. She was beautiful, intellectual, and an accomplished musician and sportswoman. Conan Doyle also loved the fact that Jean was reputed to be related to romantic Scottish hero Rob Roy. Their attraction was intense and they continued to meet discreetly. The relationship remained secret until Touie's death in 1906.

Above: American actor William Gillette was the only player to have his characterization of Sherlock Holmes endorsed by Conan Doyle.

Conan Doyle's literary life was to be interrupted by the Boer War (1899–1902). He was determined to join up as a soldier. Aged forty, out of shape, and overweight, Doyle was deemed unfit to enlist. He therefore volunteered to serve as a medical doctor and sailed to Africa in February 1900, where he worked for the volunteer-staffed Langman Field Hospital in Bloemfontein as an unofficial supervisor.

The war itself had been inspired by the desire of the British High Commissioner of South Africa's Cape Colony to take control of the gold mines of the Transvaal and Orange Free State. The Boer (ethnic Dutch) settlers to the region were in possession of these hugely valuable assets.

Right: In 1897 Conan Doyle met the attractive and accomplished Miss Jean Leckie, who was to become his second wife in 1907.

Although the British ultimately overpowered the far weaker Boer opposition, the War proved disastrous for them as well. Despite their massive military superiority, the guerrilla tactics of the Boer fighters inflicted terrible losses on the British Army, which resulted in savage reprisals. These included the confinement of many Boer women and children in the first ever concentration camps, where at least 25,000 innocent non-combatants and wounded Boer fighters were to die of starvation and disease. Conan Doyle and the other medical staff spent the war trying to save the British forces from the scourge of typhoid, which killed far more men than did the Boer fighters.

Left: Conan Doyle in medical corps uniform during the Boer War. He was fiercely patriotic and volunteered to serve.

Below: Conan Doyle was affected by what he had seen in South Africa and he wrote a book attempting to justify Britain's involvement in the conflict. Most believed that he owed his knighthood to this "patriotic" work.

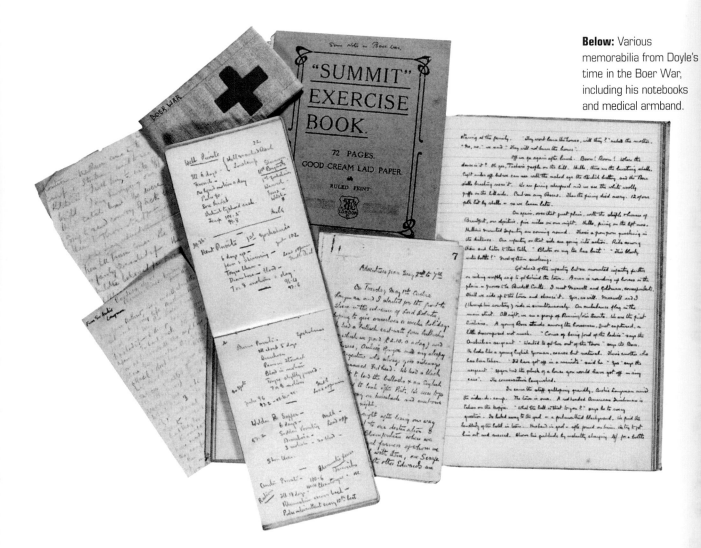

Below: Various memorabilia from Doyle's time in the Boer War, including his notebooks and medical armband.

Although the British forces ultimately triumphed, their victory came at an enormous cost. International opinion was appalled by the outrages that the British had perpetrated against other European settlers, and the large number of dead and wounded soldiers turned domestic public opinion against the British Imperial tradition.

Conan Doyle's epic work, *The Great Boer War* (1900), and *The War in South Africa: Its Causes and Conduct*, which he had published two years later, were explorations of British military failure, and an attempt to justify British involvement in the conflict. It is widely believed that he owed his knighthood to these works, rather than to his great commercial success. Partly for this reason, Conan Doyle was extremely reluctant to accept the honor. But when his mother pointed out that to refuse it would be to insult the King (Edward VII), Conan Doyle reluctantly accepted the accolade. He was knighted at Buckingham Palace, London in August 1902. Although Conan Doyle's contribution to the nation's war effort may have been the official reason for which he was awarded the knighthood, it was rumored that the King hoped the honor would encourage him to write more Sherlock Holmes stories. In the same year,

Although Conan Doyle's contribution to the nation's war effort may have been the official reason for which he was awarded the knighthood, it was rumored that the King hoped the honor would encourage him to write more Sherlock Holmes stories.

Conan Doyle was also appointed Deputy-Lieutenant of Surrey, his home county.

Like many returning participants in the Boer War, Conan Doyle came home a disillusioned man, and became far more politically motivated. In 1900, he ran for a parliamentary seat in Central Edinburgh (1900), in the "premier Radical stronghold of Scotland," as a Liberal Unionist. Although he was ultimately unsuccessful, Conan Doyle lost respectably, by a narrow margin of votes.

Far more successful than Doyle's forays into politics was his return to writing about Holmes. Legend has it that he and his close friend Bertram Fletcher Robinson came up with a brilliant new plot for Holmes while on a golfing holiday in Cromer, Norfolk (they were staying at the Royal Links Hotel). The men had met on board ship in 1900, traveling back from Cape Town, where Robinson had been working as a foreign correspondent for *The Daily Express* newspaper. Their talk of the windswept Devonshire moors at Dartmoor, the area's rich folklore, and its infamously bleak prison helped the pair conjure a terrifying spectral hound that only the most famous detective in the world could lay to rest. The *Strand* published the first episode of the novel that was to become *The Hound of the Baskervilles* in August 1901. The completed novel was released on March 25, 1902. When it was published, Conan Doyle wrote to Robison, giving him full credit for his input, "your account of a west country legend which first suggested the idea of this little tale to mind. For that, and for the help which you gave me in its evolution, all thanks." There is also speculation that Robinson also helped Conan Doyle to plot the book.

For Conan Doyle, the period between 1903 and 1906 was one of mixed fortunes. Professionally, these years were very active. The huge success of *The Hound of the Baskervilles* led to American publishers offering $5,000 apiece for Holmes stories, and to Conan Doyle becoming the most highly paid author in history to this point. Huge financial offers from his American and English publishers drove Conan Doyle back to working with his most successful creation. A new Holmes series, *The Return of Sherlock Holmes*, began in the October issue of the *Strand*. It concluded in December 1904 with "The Second Stain." The stories were published in book form in 1905. Another serial, *Sir Nigel*, also appeared in the *Strand* in December 1905, and concluded in the December 1906 issue.

The success of his literary work did not touch all areas of Conan

Doyle's life. He stood as the Liberal Unionist candidate for another parliamentary seat (Hawick District) in the General Election of spring 1906 and lost. There was still worse to come. Touie died in his arms on July 4, 1906. Although Conan Doyle had been in love with Jean Leckie for many years, he had continued to have a deep affection for his wife. He was devastated by her loss and became seriously depressed.

For Doyle, one way out of depression was to involve himself in a "cause." The George Edalji case was the first of many. Edalji was a lawyer who had been convicted of the bizarre charge of cattle maiming in 1903. Conan Doyle discovered that the man's eyesight was far too poor for a safe conviction, and in any case, the mutilations had continued after his incarceration. Edalji was acquitted in May 1907, and the case led to the establishment of the Court of Criminal Appeal, designed to correct other miscarriages of justice.

Perhaps the most famous cause in which Conan Doyle became involved was the long-running Oscar Slater case. Slater, an immigrant German Jew, was convicted of the 1909 brutal murder of wealthy eighty-two-year-old Glaswegian widow Marion Gilchrist. It came to light that Gilchrist was almost certainly murdered by a member of her own (highly respectable) family. Oscar Slater, who led a disreputable life as a pimp and gambler, was framed for the crime to protect Scotland's social elite.

Complicity in this cover-up stretched into the very highest levels of the Scottish legal system. Conan Doyle studied the case thoroughly and published The Case of Oscar Slater in 1912. Despite a vigorous campaign to free the wrongly accused, Slater was to endure eighteen years' hard labor before new evidence that Conan Doyle placed before British Prime Minister J. Ramsay MacDonald led to his release in 1927. Although £6,000 was paid in compensation to Oscar Slater for the appalling suffering he had endured, his name was never formally cleared, and the guilty parties were never brought to justice. Even so, Slater was enormously grateful to Conan Doyle for the

Left: George Edalji was one of several convicted, but innocent, men that Conan Doyle attempted to clear. By using Holmesian methods of deduction, Conan Doyle was able to prove that the Edalji's eyesight was too poor to have committed his "crimes" at night.

Right: Another celebrated case in which Doyle played a leading part was the Oscar Slater affair. Convicted of murder, Slater had already spent eighteen years in jail when Conan Doyle secured his release in 1927. Conan Doyle presented the facts to the Prime Minister, Ramsay MacDonald.

quashing of his sentence in 1928, and wrote to thank the "breaker of my shackles."

On September 18, 1907, Conan Doyle married Jean Leckie at St. Margaret's Church, Westminster. In contrast to their clandestine courtship, the marriage was a very public affair, taking place in front of 250 guests. The happy couple moved to a new home, Windelsham, in Crowborough, Sussex, England, together with Arthur's first two children from his marriage to Touie. Conan Doyle was to spend the rest of his life living in this house, keeping just a small pied a terre in London.

Following his happy second marriage, Conan Doyle's literary output was somewhat reduced. He wrote three indifferent plays, the staging of which involved him in heavy financial losses. Determined to recoup the money, Conan Doyle decided to write a play that would be a sure-fire

success, one featuring his best-loved creation. *The Stonor Case* was based on the Holmes story "The Adventure of the Speckled Band." (Published as "The Spotted Band" in the New York World, this was Conan Doyle's favorite Sherlock short story.) The play, which featured a live python, opened at London's Adelphi Theatre and received rave reviews, running for 346 performances. Conan Doyle's losses were more than recouped. At this point, the author very wisely decided to retire from "stage work," concerned that his great interest in this medium might involve further fiscal failure.

The next few years were happy ones, both personally and professionally. Jean and Arthur became parents three times. Denis Percy Stewart Conan was born in 1909, Adrian Malcolm Conan in 1910, and Jean Lena Annette Conan in 1912. Several more Holmes stories were published in the *Strand*, which also published stories about a completely new Conan Doyle character, Professor Challenger, between April and November 1912. The first Challenger novel, *The Lost World*, appeared in October 1912. A new book, *The Valley of Fear* was serialized in 1914 and 1915. It was the fourth and final full-length novel featuring Homes.

Conan Doyle was involved in several public campaigns during this period. He became President of the Divorce Law Reform Union in 1909, and began to fight against the oppressive regime in the Belgian Congo. He also joined the campaign supporting a channel tunnel between England and France. Contemporary naval experts described this objective as a "Jules Verne fantasy."

A second North American tour took up most of the summer of 1914. The Conan Doyles arrived in New York aboard the RMS *Olympic* on May 27. Conan Doyle's writings, especially his Sherlock Holmes stories, were

Above: Just like Holmes, Conan Doyle was to spend many happy years in proximity to the English South Downs, at Windelsham near Crowborough, Sussex.

Above: A photograph of Jean Conan Doyle with the couple's two young sons. Sir Arthur often carried the photograph with him.

popular in the United States and Canada, and Holmes plays that started their runs on Broadway toured the major cities of the entire continent. The tour was inspired by an invitation to Jasper Park from the Canadian Government, but he also took the opportunity to visit various places of interest in New York (including Sing Sing prison) before traveling on to Montreal, the Great Lakes, Fort William, Winnipeg, Edmonton, Niagara Falls, and Ottawa. His tour included the delivery of a lecture, "The Future of Canadian Literature," which he gave in Montreal on June 4, 1914. Interestingly, Conan Doyle also gave his audience a glimpse into his own writing technique, stressing the importance of the author constantly improving his general knowledge with continual reading. He also read his own newly composed poem about the beauty of the Canadian wilderness, "The Athabasca Trail," at the Canadian Club of Ottawa on July 2, 1914. The Conan Doyles set sail to return to Liverpool on July 4, aboard the RMS *Megantic*.

Even during these happy times, there was an undercurrent of looming danger in Conan Doyle's writing. He was convinced that a European war was inevitable. His last stories have menacing echoes of German insurgency, and in "His Last Bow," Holmes speak of the "east wind coming. It will be cold and bitter, Watson, and a good many of us may

Above: A copy of the first American edition of Doyle's book warning Britain about the dangers of Germany's foreign policies. It was published in 1913.

Left: Conan Doyle meeting with Houdini during an American tour of the 1920s.

wither before its blast" Like many informed men of his generation, Conan Doyle was extremely concerned that Britain was not militarily prepared for such a conflict. He was also apprehensive of how the country would deal with new German inventions, such as the submarine and airship. In February 1913, he wrote an article for the Fortnightly Review entitled "Britain and the Next War," and the Strand published "Danger!" in July 1914. This was a warning of the potentially devastating effects of a wartime blockade. When war broke out in August 1914, Conan Doyle immediately offered to enlist, but was turned down once again. He was by now fifty-five. Ironically, he describes how Watson joins up with his "old service," although the fictional doctor must be sixty-two. In 1916, Conan Doyle enlisted as a private in the Volunteer Battalion of the Royal Sussex Regiment. His daughter, Mary, also became involved in the war effort, volunteering at Peel House, where troops leaving for the front were served with home comforts.

Throughout the conflict, Conan Doyle kept up a continual

Above: Conan Doyle's barrage of suggestions on how to save the lives of the military fell on deaf ears for the most part. Only Winston Churchill had the sense to thank him for his fresh ideas.

correspondence with the British military authorities, suggesting ways in which the lives of fighting men could be saved. These included issuing sailors with "inflatable rubber belts" and supplying front line fighters with body armor. Today, most of his suggestions seem obvious, but the authorities found his naïve enthusiasm little more than irritating. Only the young Winston Churchill wrote to thank Conan Doyle for his fresh ideas.

Conan Doyle visited both the British and French frontlines in 1916, and was absolutely appalled by the awful bloodshed he witnessed, the "tangle of mutilated horses, their necks rising and sinking," amid the remains of fallen soldiers. He wrote a series of articles about his experiences, *The British Campaign in France and Flanders: 1914*, which appeared in the *Strand* during from April 1916 to June 1917. The following year, the government was so concerned by the effect of his powerful writing might have that they censored his history of the campaign.

As a rather strange footnote to Conan Doyle's unstinting patriotism, the Germans were also quick to spot the morale-boosting values of his most successful creation. Fifteen Holmes films were released in Germany during the conflict.

1917 saw the publication of another Holmes collection of stories that had appeared episodically in the *Strand*, when John Murray published *His Last Bow*. In contrast to The Valley of Fear, the book was very well received.

Like so many British families, the Conan Doyles were to reap a terrible harvest from the war. Arthur's eldest son, Captain Kingsley Conan Doyle, died from influenza aggravated by war wounds in 1918, while his brother, Brigadier-General Innes Doyle, succumbed to post-war pneumonia the following year. Conan Doyle also lost two brothers-in-law, including Malcolm Leckie, and two nephews in the conflict. "The Ma'am" also died in 1920. These multiple shocks had a very profound effect on Conan Doyle. He became obsessed with the occult and Spiritualism, and spent the enormous sum of over a quarter of a million pounds trying to prove that it was possible to communicate with the dead. This desire was undoubtedly fueled by his dreadful sense of loss, which must have been shared by millions, but he had maintained an interest in spirituality for many years, since his rejection of his Roman Catholic faith when he left school.

His interest in spiritualism actually pre-dated these family tragedies. He had publicly declared himself to be a Spiritualist in 1916, in an article for the Spiritualist magazine, Light, in which he also announced his belief in communication with the dead. In 1917, he had also begun to lecture for the "cause." But following Kingsley's death, his attendance at séances became increasingly regular, and according to Conan Doyle, he heard the voice of his son on at least one occasion. Perhaps their controversial beliefs led the Doyles to draw even closer together as a family, and Conan Doyle's mother moved south from Yorkshire to be near her son.

Despite his wife's initial repugnance for Spiritualism, which she considered "uncanny and dangerous," Jean Conan Doyle began to share her husband's beliefs after the war-death of her brother Malcolm. With her husband's encouragement, Jean also began to explore her talent for "trance-writing." Conan Doyle himself was particularly interested in the phenomenon of "spirit photographs" showing "ectoplasmic hands" and other apparitions. He himself appears in many photographs in this genre. His ultimate aim was to join the branches of the Christian church together in a "new church" whose main preoccupations would be contact with the dead and reunion of the dead with the living.

Unfortunately, Conan Doyle's strong desire for proof of the ethereal world resulted in public ridicule for his involvement in the affair of the Cottingley Fairies. Two young girls, Elsie Wright and her cousin, Frances Griffiths, had taken several photographs in July and September 1917 that seemed to show the girls surrounded by a crown of dancing fairies. Although the photographs were received with a good deal of skepticism, Conan Doyle gradually came to the belief that they were proof of a world peopled by fairies and other "little folk." Although it may sound ridiculous to modern readers, a belief in fairies, elves, gnomes, and sprites was not

Left: Conan Doyle and his wife Jean during their spiritualist period. They are seen here with Charles Richet, a renowned French spiritualist. The famous postcard shows Elsie Wright, a young girl from Yorkshire, pictured surrounded by fairies. Amazingly, Conan Doyle accepted this amateur fake as proof of the existence of these fey creatures.

Above: Frances Griffiths, Elsie Wright's cousin, was also involved in the Cottingley Fairies affair. She is pictured talking to a gnome.

unusual at this time. Conan Doyle's own uncle, Richard ("Dick") Doyle had made a name for himself illustrating fairy folk for *Punch* magazine and several books, including *The Fairy Ring*, a collection of Grimm's fairy stories. Dick's reputation for drawing the "little folk" grew, and author William Thackeray hailed him as the "new master of fairyland." More bizarrely, the incarcerated Charles Doyle also filled page after page of his drawing notebook with fantasy figures, which he believed he was drawing from life.

Fueled by intense public interest, the *Strand* published the rather beautiful Cottingley photographs, and asked Conan Doyle to write an article about fairies for the Christmas 1920 issue. Conan Doyle believed that the photographs were genuine, and proved the existence of a parallel, spirit world, that brought a "glamour and mystery to life." He expanded these views in his 1922 book, *The Coming of the Fairies*. Although many contemporaries were also convinced of the authenticity of the pictures, many others could not understand how the creator of the great logician, Sherlock Holmes, could be taken in by a transparent, girlish prank. The great author's reputation suffered as a result. It was not until 1983 that Elsie Wright finally confirmed that the "fairies" she had photographed had been cut out of magazines and stuck on hatpins. Her confession also proved beyond contradiction that Conan Doyle had been duped by two schoolgirls.

The mockery Conan Doyle suffered over the Cottingley Fairies episode did nothing to sway his belief in Spiritualism. He often spoke of his occult experiences, including touching phantom hands and conversations he had had with the dead. Between 1920 and 1930, the entire Conan Doyle family embarked on a worldwide crusade to further the Spiritualist cause. They visited Australia, Europe, South Africa, Kenya, and Rhodesia. In 1923, they traveled to the United States, attempting to start a new "Church of America." The Conan Doyles toured the country, from east to west coast, preaching their cause and showing hundreds of their "spirit photographs." Many of these had been taken by William Hope of Crewe, England, and by modern standards, appear to be nothing more than blatant and obvious fakes. The Conan Doyles made great efforts to counter the ingrained skepticism they were met with; "Nothing is as dogmatic as science," Conan Doyle maintained. It was during this trip that he struck up a strange friendship with Harry Houdini, the famous illusionist. Both were completely fascinated by Spiritualism. But while Conan Doyle was completely engrossed with trying to prove the existence of the "spirit world," Houdini was just as anxious to expose "mediumistic parlor tricks." For a while they maintained a close relationship, but a rift developed and the ensuing squabble ended only with Houdini's death in 1926.

Conan Doyle wrote an immense number of books and articles, trying to prove the validity of his occult interests. With few exceptions, these were nothing more than a drain on his financial resources. Perhaps the most famous of these was *The Land of Mist*, a novel of psychic adventures, published in March 1925. Conan Doyle also opened a "psychic bookshop" and spirit museum on London's Victoria Street, in the shadow of Westminster Abbey. Mary Doyle, Conan Doyle's daughter from his first marriage, ran the shop. During this period, his Spiritualist beliefs were his all-consuming interest. "I might play with a steam yacht or own racehorses. I prefer to do this," he said.

Above: Conan Doyle in later years, enjoying his pipe.

The effect of his obsession with the occult was by no means entirely benign. Many members of his loyal public came to think of the famed author as foolish and credulous, and he lost several valued friends, including Sax Rohmer (the creator of Fu Manchu and the author of *The Romance of Sorcery*).

Conan Doyle's Spiritualist "work" brought in little or no money, and the family's proselytizing crusades were expensive. In 1927, John Murray published the final collection of twelve new Holmes stories, *The Case-Book of Sherlock Holmes*, which brought in some much-needed income. These stories were the second reincarnation of Holmes that Conan Doyle was obliged to make for financial reasons. He was thoroughly irritated by this necessity and asserted that the renowned detective would not reappear again in any circumstances whatsoever. The great detective's "retirement" led to several elderly ladies writing to offer their housekeeping services.

The family's income was further bolstered in October 1928, when Murray published a collection of his Sherlockian oeuvre, *The Complete Sherlock Holmes Short Stories*. In June 1929, his non- Sherlockian work was also collected into a single volume and published by Murray as *The Conan Doyle Stories*. In July, they released what turned out to be Conan Doyle's final collection of new fiction, *The Maracot Deep and Other Stories*. The income from these publications funded a renewed Spiritualist crusade. His final psychic tour, in the autumn of 1929, took him to Holland, Denmark, Norway, and Sweden.

Conan Doyle's health had been on the decline through the 1920s (he had suffered several minor heart attacks) and seemed further undermined by the strain of this final tour and by a serious cold he had caught in Scandinavia. He had to be carried ashore on his return to England, and was subsequently diagnosed with angina pectoris. This proved to be a terminal condition, and he died the following year, at home at Windlesham, at 8:30 a.m. on Monday, July 7, 1930. He was seventy-one. As the man who had once been described as "the most prominent living Englishman" lay on his deathbed, his close and loving family surrounded

Above: The author as a young man, almost certainly in the 1880s, when he was just starting out on the road to become an author.

Opposite: Conan Doyle's final resting place in Minstead Churchyard, Hampshire, England.

him. Only Mary, his eldest daughter was missing. (This may well be telling. Recent work seems to indicate that a rift had grown up between father and daughter, possibly due to some pressure brought by his second wife. May was certainly cut out of a share in his royalties under the terms of his will.) His son, Adrian Doyle, commended his father's bravery in the face of death, "I have never seen anyone take anything more gamely in all my life. Even when we knew he was suffering great pain, he always managed to keep a smile for us." His final words were addressed to Jean, who had patiently nursed her husband for the final months of his life, "You are wonderful," he said.

For the Conan Doyle family, this could not be the end. Although he had departed on the "greatest and most glorious adventure of all," they fully expected that he would communicate with them from beyond the grave. "I know perfectly well I am going to have conversations with my father," maintained Adrian Conan Doyle. Mediums everywhere waited anxiously for Conan Doyle's messages from "beyond the veil," and his image began to appear in a flurry of dubious "spirit photographs."

A few days after his death, his family buried Conan Doyle near the garden hut at Windelsham, which he had so often used as a study. He had a simple oak marker, inscribed, at Jean's insistence, with just his name, date of birth, and a four-word motto. The words were borrowed from Robert Louis Stephenson:

> *Steel True*
> *Blade Straight*
> *ARTHUR CONAN DOYLE*
> *Knight*
> *22 May 1859 – 7 July 1930*

In the light of their Spiritualist beliefs, the Conan Doyles refused any outward show of mourning, and Jean wore a flowered summer dress.

This certainly seems a strange end for a man whose chief creation, the cornerstone of his great reputation, was the very personification of logical deduction based on the application of intellect and evidence. But as Conan Doyle had already told us, "the created is not the creator . . . The doll and its maker are never identical."

CHAPTER TWO

Sherlock Holmes: A Life in Print

· ·
·

The first editions of Conan Doyle's Sherlockian stories appeared over a protracted period of forty years. Holmes was the perfect detective for a rationalist age. All were published during the author's lifetime. Several were also translated, and as well as being well known on both sides of the Atlantic, Sherlock Holmes had many European devotees. His fan base is now worldwide and there are Sherlockian Societies everywhere, including Japan, Russia, Australia, and India.

Despite the phenomenal success of the stories during Conan Doyle's lifetime, since his death, an even more extraordinary publishing phenomenon has evolved. Not only have all the stories remained in print since they were first launched, but there is also a burgeoning market for Sherlockian literary collectibles of every description. Holmes bibliophiles collect a vast array of literary material featuring the great detective, some

"It is very much the sort of thing that I expected" said he "Of course we do not yet know what the relations may have been between Alec Cunningham, William Kirwan, and Annie Morrison. The result shows that the trap was skilfully baited. I am sure that you cannot fail to be delighted with the traces of heredity shown in the ps and in the tails of the qs. The absence of the i-dots in the old man's writing is also most characteristic. Watson, I think our quiet rest in the country has been a distinct success, and I shall certainly return much invigorated to Baker Street tomorrow.

Opposite: A fragment of manuscript in the author's handwriting contains the final eleven lines of the Sherlock Holmes Story *The Adventure of the Reigate Squires.*

The American actor, William Gillette, was the first artist closely identified with the role of Holmes, but many other distinguished actors followed in his footsteps, including Basil Rathbone, John Geilgud, John Barrymore, Jeremy Brett, and Peter Cushing. It is said that more actors have played Sherlock Holmes than any other literary character.

A Study in Scarlet

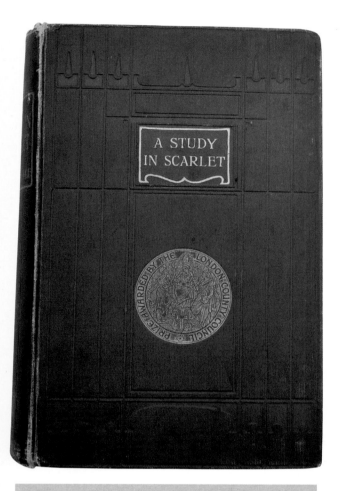

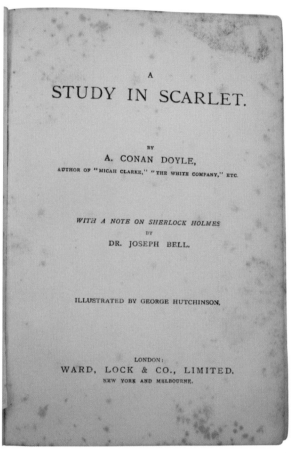

A
STUDY IN SCARLET.

BY
A. CONAN DOYLE,
AUTHOR OF "MICAH CLARKE," "THE WHITE COMPANY," ETC.

WITH A NOTE ON SHERLOCK HOLMES
BY
DR. JOSEPH BELL.

ILLUSTRATED BY GEORGE HUTCHINSON.

LONDON:
WARD, LOCK & CO., LIMITED.
NEW YORK AND MELBOURNE.

A STUDY IN SCARLET.
London : Ward, Lock & Co., Ltd.

First Edition (as Beeton's Christmas Annual)			.	1887
Second Edition. Crown 8vo	.	. .	.	1888
Reprinted .	. . .	. .	.	1889
Third Edition. Crown 8vo. Illustrated		.	.	1891
Reprinted. Crown 8vo. Illustrated	,	.	.	1892
,,	,,	,,	. .	1892
,,	,,	,,	. .	1892
,,	,,	,,	. .	1892
,,	,,	,, With Note on Sherlock Holmes by Dr. Jos. Bell		1893
,,	,,	,,	,,	1894
Fourth Edition. Royal 8vo.	,,	,,	,,	1895
Reprinted. Crown 8vo.	,,	,,	,,	1896
,,	,,	,,	,,	1898
Fifth Edition. Crown 8vo.	,,	,,	,,	1899
Reprinted	,,	,,	,,	1901
,,	,,	,,	,,	1902
,,	,,	,,	,,	1902
,,	,,	,,	,,	1904
Sixth Edition. Demy 8vo.	,,	,,		1902
Reprinted. Demy 8vo.		,,	,,	1902
,,	,,	,,	,,	1903
,,	,,	,,	,,	1904

Left: The author's copy of Ward Lock's 1904 edition of *A Study In Scarlet*. It was awarded to his grandfather as a school prize in 1905, and is illustrated by George Hutchinson. The copyright page shows that this edition of the book had already reprinted twenty-one times in seventeen years. Notes by Dr. Joseph Bell were added in 1893. It is significant that although written as popular fiction, the Sherlock Holmes stories were deemed sufficiently "educational" to be given as school prizes. It has an embossed blue cloth binding, which is stamped in gold leaf.

of which (especially rare and first editions) have become extremely valuable. Shakespeare's Hamlet is said to be the only other fictional character to have generated a partially comparable "personality" cult. In addition to the enormous number of published editions of the works themselves, there is a massive array of other literary genres featuring Conan Doyle's creation. These include critical essays, spoof Holmes adventures, "biographies" of various Sherlockian characters, illustrated novels, comic books, Conan Doyle pastiches, condensed versions, and biographies of the author himself.

As well as the many private individuals nurturing large and specialized Holmes collections, such as the magnificent collection of Sherlockiana and original manuscripts amassed by Doctor C. Frederick Kittle, there are also public assemblages. The Toronto Reference Library and the University of Minnesota Libraries both have extraordinary collections of material about Conan Doyle and Sherlock, which is accessible to the public. The Toronto Reference Library houses a vast array of both primary and secondary source material, and has recently acquired an extraordinary set of manuscripts and documents that feature Conan Doyle's connections to "Canada and the Empire."

Toronto's Arthur Conan Doyle Collection also encompasses stage and screen adaptations of the Sherlockian works. This is particularly relevant, as it was only a few years following their original composition that Conan Doyle's stories were brought to life on stage, and only a couple of decades until Holmes and Watson appeared on screen. The American actor, William Gillette, was the first artist closely identified with the role of Holmes, but many other distinguished actors followed in his footsteps, including Basil Rathbone, John Geilgud, John Barrymore, Jeremy Brett, and Peter Cushing. It is said that more actors have played Sherlock Holmes than any other literary character. The Marylebone Library in London also possesses a substantial Sherlock Holmes Collection. The Library's aim is to collect as much material as possible about both the great detective and his creator, and to make it freely available. Their collection includes several rarities, including Conan Doyle's original manuscripts of "The Dying Detective" and "The Lion's Mane."

Other collectors specialize in acquiring the translated editions of Conan Doyle's Holmesian oeuvre. It is estimated that the stories appear in eighty-two different languages, including Braille, several obscure Indian dialects (including Teluga, Kannada, Oriya, and Sindhi), Azeri, Cyrillic, Hindi, Mongolian, Pitman Shorthand, Dancing Men, Esperanto, and Pig Latin.

The Holy Grail for the Sherlock bibliophile is the first published edition of the very first tale. The great detective first materialized in *Beeton's Christmas Annual* for 1887 in the story, "A Study in Scarlet." The magazine still bore the name of its original publisher, Sam Beeton (husband of the famous cookery writer Mrs. Beeton), but by this time the masthead was owned by Ward, Lock & Co. *Beeton's Christmas Annual* had

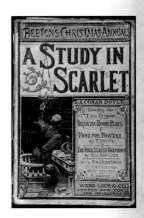

Above: *A Study in Scarlet* first appeared in Beeton's Christmas Annual for 1887. Copies of this edition are extremely prized by collectors, and very valuable.

Right and Opposite: The popularity of Sherlock Holmes's adventures guaranteed that they would be translated into many languages, as these two dramatic Spanish-language magazine covers demonstrate.

N.° 34

Memorias íntimas de SHERLOCK HOLMES

Sherlock Holmes y el contrabandista de opio

Cuchillo en mano se dirigió el de la barba negra hacia Sherlock Holmes, que pendía del techo atado eu él por los pies.

a color picture "wrapper," and was priced at a modest shilling. It was highly successful and sold out well before that Christmas. Original copies of this issue are now among the most valuable magazines in literary history. In June 2007, Sotheby's of New York sold a copy of the magazine for $156,000, despite the fact that it was creased, worn, and had a small hole in the front wrapper.

Even during his lifetime, several translated versions of Conan Doyle's Sherlock stories were published, but his original, and perhaps most important audience, remained either side of the Atlantic. *A Study in Scarlet*, volume form, appeared in 1888, published by Ward, Lock & Co.

N.º 38

Memorias íntimas de SHERLOCK HOLMES

En la escuela del crimen de Pittsburg

Cuando el malhechor iba á clavar el puñal en el corazón de Harry Taxon, acercóse de súbito Sherlock Holmes y le agarró con mano férrea por el brazo.

This set the pattern for the publication of almost all of the Sherlock Holmes stories in Great Britain, and meant that Conan Doyle was paid at least twice for all his published work.

But Conan Doyle's most important publishing relationship was with the *Strand* magazine. His literary agent, A. P. Watt, who made a deal with the *Strand* to publish Conan Doyle's first six Sherlock Holmes short stories, initiated this partnership. Starting with "A Scandal in Bohemia" in July 1891, they continued to publish first editions of his Sherlock Holmes stories until "Shoscombe Old Place" in April 1927. A complete set of original *Strand* magazines in which the illustrated stories first appeared would be an extremely rare and desirable item of "Sherlockiana."

The first edition of the *Strand* had appeared in January 1891. Founded by publisher George Newnes, the magazine was aimed at a middle class family audience, and became the most popular and important periodical of the day. Its winning formula consisted of a lively mixture of fiction, current affairs, and informative articles, complete with "a picture on every page." The *Strand* was priced at a humble sixpence, half the price of most similar publications, and was published monthly. Conan Doyle deliberately tailored his writing to the publishing format of the magazine, and his work appeared in almost every monthly issue until his death in 1930. This was a hugely beneficial relationship that made a fortune for both parties. The *Strand* itself survived until 1950. Besides Conan Doyle, its famous contributors included Queen Victoria, Winston Churchill, D. H. Lawrence, G. K. Chesterton, Leo Tolstoy, H. G. Wells,

Left and above: Two Spanish versions of the German-language pastiches of the Holmes stories, which were first published in 1907. They were printed in the "nickel thriller" format and remained in print, selling to Spanish-speaking Americans, until the 1980s.

THE STRAND MAGAZINE.

Vol. xxiii.　　　　　　　　　　APRIL, 1902　　　　　　　　　　No. 136.

The Hound of the Baskervilles.

ANOTHER ADVENTURE OF
SHERLOCK HOLMES

By CONAN DOYLE.

" HOLMES EMPTIED FIVE BARRELS OF HIS REVOLVER INTO THE
CREATURE'S FLANK."

Left: The *Strand* published the first editions of the Holmes stories between 1891 and 1927. Conan Doyle tailored his writing to fit the format of the magazine. Here is the April 1902 edition, featuring *The Hound of the Baskervilles* with Sidney Paget's illustrations.

Agatha Christie, and mystery writer Margery Allingham.

In volume form, Conan Doyle's work appeared on the lists of several reputable British companies. Spencer Blackett published *The Sign of Four* in 1890, while George Newnes, Ltd. published *The Adventures of Sherlock Holmes* (1892), *The Memoirs of Sherlock Holmes* (1894), *The Hound of the Baskervilles* (1902), and *The Return of Sherlock Holmes* (1905). Smith, Elder & Co. of London became Conan Doyle's volume publisher in 1915 with the release of *The Valley of Fear*, but with the launch of *His Last Bow* in 1917, Conan Doyle moved to John Murray (of London). Murray also published his final volumes, *The Case-Book of Sherlock Holmes* (1927), *The Complete Short Stories of Sherlock Holmes* (1929), and *The Complete Long Stories of Sherlock Holmes* (1929).

Just as in the UK, many Conan Doyle stories were first published in America in serial form, appearing in various magazines, then re-launched in volume form. Once published, the stories often fell victim to America's rather loose copyright laws. The work of Conan Doyle, Wilkie Collins, and Charles Dickens was all republished without their consent, or (far worse) any payment. Charles Dickens particularly resented the loss of income that this infringement caused. An American copyright law was introduced in 1891, but it did not cover material already published, and pirate editions of Conan Doyle's work continued to appear until 1930.

Below:

Philadelphia–based *Lippincott's Monthly Magazine* was one of the first publishers to feature the Holmes stories in the United States.

Conan Doyle's first American publisher was J. B. Lippincott and Co. of Philadelphia and New York, who published *A Study in Scarlet* in book form in 1890. Bookstall operators Benjamin Warner and Jacob Johnson had founded the company in Philadelphia in 1792. By the mid-nineteenth century, it was one of the biggest publishers in the English-speaking world. But while J. B. Lippincott picked up a story that had already been published in England, magazine proprietor Joseph Marshall Stoddart commissioned *The Sign of Four*, to be serialized in his *Lippincott's Monthly Magazine*. The magazine was published in Philadelphia between 1868 and 1915, when it relocated to New York and became *McBride's Magazine*. As well as publishing Conan Doyle, Lippincott's also published Rudyard Kipling's *The Light that Failed* and Oscar Wilde's *Picture of Dorian Gray*.

With the 1892 publication of *The Adventures of Sherlock Holmes*, Harper's Weekly took over the role of Conan Doyle's magazine publisher in America. Fletcher Harper founded the magazine in 1857, impressed by the success of the *Illustrated London News*.

McClure's Magazine published several Conan Doyle stories, beginning with "The Final Problem" in December 1893. Irish-American Samuel Sidney McClure had founded the magazine that year, and sold it at a reduced price of fifteen cents an issue. McClure's also published other

IN THIS NUMBER—"THE RETURN OF SHERLOCK HOLMES"

Beginning a New Series of Detective Stories by A. CONAN DOYLE

Collier's

Household Number for October

VOL XXXI NO 26   SEPTEMBER 26 1903   PRICE IC CENTS

Left: It was *Collier's* that was to become most closely associated with publishing the Holmes stories in magazine form for American readers. Frederic Dorr Steele's highly distinctive illustrations graced *Collier's* covers.

prominent authors of the day, including Rudyard Kipling.

It was *Collier's Weekly* that was responsible for introducing most of the Sherlockian "middle canon" to America. Peter Fendon Collier had founded the magazine in 1888, and it had been almost immediately successful, quickly building a monthly circulation of around 250,000 copies. At the time, this was one of the largest in America. Collier's began their association with Conan Doyle in February 1893 with the publication

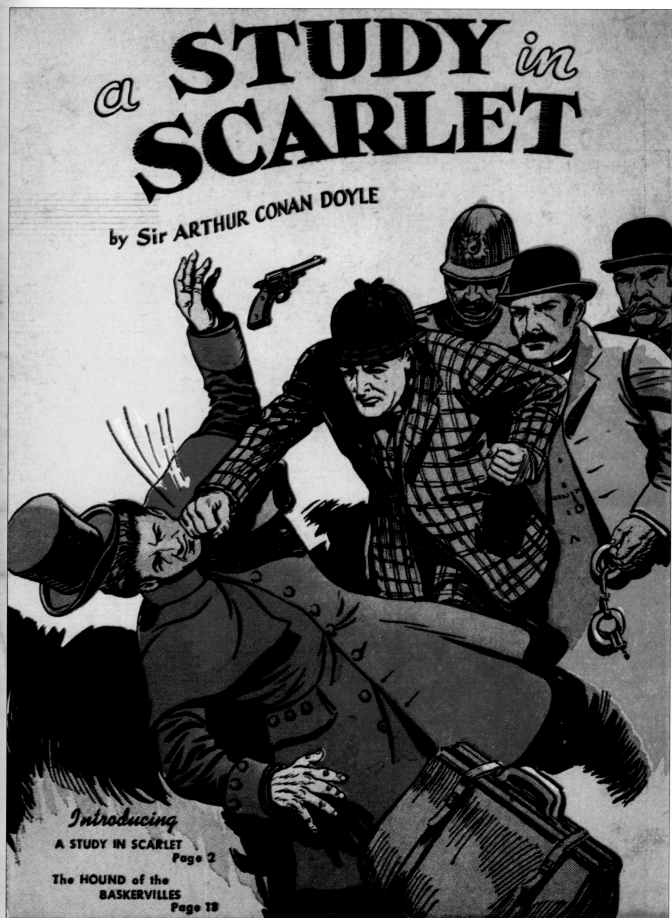

of "Silver Blaze," and continued to publish new Holmes stories until "The Illustrious Client" appeared in November 1924.

The American Magazine, Hearst's International, and (to a far greater extent) *Liberty* magazine were responsible for serializing the later Sherlock works in America. *The American Magazine* published just one Holmes story, "The Disappearance of Lady Frances Carfax" in 1911. The magazine was founded by ex-*McClure's Magazine* staff in 1906 and became a feature of the American literary landscape until it failed half a century later, in 1956. Hearst's *International* was originated by an Episcopal bishop in 1901, and was acquired by William Randolph Hearst in 1912. It retained its devotion to current affairs, but with an admixture of fiction. Between 1921 and 1924, the magazine published four original Sherlock Holmes stories. *Liberty* started publication in 1924, and was said to be the "second greatest magazine in America," only less popular than the massively successful *Saturday Evening Post*. It was a general interest publication, but also published fiction by the finest writers of the period, including Sherlock Holmes stories (in 1926 and 1927), and the early novels of P. G. Wodehouse.

In volume form, Conan Doyle's work appeared on a number of American publishers' lists. J. B. Lippincott Co. was the first (*A Study in Scarlet*, 1890). The next was P. F. Collier, who published *The Sign of Four* in 1891, followed by Harper & Bros. of New York, who released *The Adventures of Sherlock Holmes* in 1892 and *The Memoirs of Sherlock Holmes* in 1894. McClure, Phillips & Co. of New York became Conan Doyle's publisher in 1902, when they released *The Hound of the Baskervilles*, and continued with *The Return of Sherlock Holmes* in 1905. George H. Doran of New York launched *The Valley of Fear* (1915), *His Last Bow* (1917), and *The Casebook of Sherlock Holmes* (1927). Doubleday, Doran & Co. of Garden City issued Conan Doyle's final collection of Holmes material as *The Complete Sherlock Holmes* in 1930.

Inevitably, the extensive number of first editions, and the plethora of re-issues and new material that has been published since Sherlock Holmes made his first appearance, have built up into an mammoth volume of collectible material. The huge interest in collecting Sherlockian literature has resulted in several bookshops and internet

Above: Samuel Sidney McClure published *The Final Problem* in his magazine in 1893, at the special price of 15 cents.

Below and opposite: Two examples of the *Classic Comics* versions of the Holmes stories, which appeared when the copyright expired in the 1940s. The cover artwork is by H.C. Keifer.

retailers that specialize in this field. Philip Gold, the proprietor of 221 Books of Westlake Village, California, has some interesting tips for anyone wanting to start a collection of Holmes books and ephemera:

"Assembling a collection of cornerstone titles will be a challenging, and perhaps a lifelong endeavor. But don't fail to inject some of your own interests and perspectives into the process. That's the secret to assembling a unique and significant collection. Books about the world's first consulting detective, Mr. Sherlock Holmes, have been a consistently popular collecting genre."

Holmesian Illustrators

"His very person and appearance were such as to strike the attention of the most casual observer. In height he was rather over six feet, and so excessively lean that he seemed to be considerably taller. His eyes were sharp and piercing . . . and his thin hawk-like nose gave his whole expression an air of smartness and decision. His chin, too, had the prominence and squareness which mark the man of decision."

Although Conan Doyle's portrait of Sherlock is highly evocative, the various illustrators that brought his work to life have made a great contribution to the indelible popular image of the great detective. At least thirty illustrators were commissioned to illustrate the English-language editions of Conan Doyle's Holmes stories during the author's lifetime. Their work has ensured that Sherlock is one of the few literary characters that is fixed in the popular imagination.

Perhaps the greatest contributor to the universal image of Holmes is Sidney Paget, who first brought Holmes to life in the *Strand*. Sidney's brother, Walter, had already illustrated Robert Louis Stevenson's *Robinson Crusoe*, and was chosen by George Newnes (the proprietor of the magazine) to work on Conan Doyle's stories. But the hand of fate intervened, and the commission was sent to Sidney in error. Conan Doyle maintained that Paget's Holmes was too good-looking, but it was Sidney that fixed the image of the detective in the public imagination, with Holmes's signature deerstalker and his distinguished, fiercely intense demeanor.

Paget was not the first illustrator to vivify the great man. D. H. Friston had drawn four illustrations for the first Holmes

Opposite: tSidney Paget's fine illustration of a rather dapper Homes and Watson in their city wear; top hats and conventional overcoats. Note that Holmes and Watson are correctly shown as being around the same age (Watson was actually two years older than Holmes). Some film characterizations depict Watson as a bumbling older man.

Below: Sidney Paget's illustration of Holmes staring into the fire in "The Five Orange Pips."

Above: Holmes and Watson examine an old oak tree with a girth of twenty-three feet in Sidney Paget's illustration for "The Musgrave Ritual."

Opposite: Paget's masterly rendition of the timely assassination of Charles Augustus Milverton.

tale, "A Study in Scarlet," for its initial publication in *Beeton's Christmas Annual*. The drawings are accomplished and moody, but while Holmes appears complete with his sideburns and caped coat, he looks far too young, fresh, and (uncharacteristically) enthusiastic. When Ward, Lock & Company reissued the story in 1888, a new set of illustrations were prepared, this time by Conan Doyle's own father, Charles Doyle. They are generally considered the worst illustrations ever to grace his work, and are very naïve, almost "cartoony." In the second edition, Ward, Lock replaced Charles Doyle's work with illustrations by George Hutchinson. But Paget became the most popular illustrator of the *Canon* in Britain, with his artistic and highly finished style. He produced 356 illustrations for thirty-eight Sherlock Holmes stories before his premature death in 1908. He also painted the famous portrait of Holmes, which appeared to have been painted from life, though this did not appear in the books themselves.

While Paget defined Holmes for British readers, a more varied set of illustrators were employed for the American editions. Over some years, a composite image of Holmes gradually emerged from the pens of artists such as W. H. Hyde, Harry Edwards, and G. Patrick Nelson.

Above: D.H. Friston's frontispiece to the 1887 version of *A Study in Scarlet* was the first ever illustration for the Holmes stories. Holmes already has his Inverness Cape and famous magnifying glass.

But it was the artist Frederic Dorr Steele who created the definitive American Holmes in his illustrations for *Collier's Weekly*. These were first published in the magazine in 1903. Steele used the famous Sherlockian actor, William Gillette, as his model for the great detective, in the same way that Paget had used his brother Walter. Of all the American illustrators of the canon, perhaps only Steele can challenge the quality of Paget's work. His image of Holmes was to endure in the American consciousness until the 1940s. Many Sherlockian scholars assert that while the original image of Holmes belongs to Paget, Steele evolved a more refined version of the man in his work. When *Harper's Weekly* took over the publication of the Sherlock Holmes stories, W. H. Hyde illustrated them. Hyde's work also has a highly finished, atmospheric quality, and compares favorably with that of both Paget and Steele.

After Paget's early death in 1908, no single British artist seemed able to assume his Holmesian mantle. For *His Last Bow,* seven different artists were commissioned to illustrate each of the seven different stories, drawing a total of forty-two pictures between them. These artists were Arthur Twiddle, Gilbert Holiday, Joseph Simpson, H. M. Brock, Alec Ball, Alfred Gilbert, and Sidney's brother, Walter Paget.

As of 1914, when the *Strand* commissioned Frank Wiles to produce thirty-two illustrations for *The Valley of Fear,* he pretty well assumed Paget's relation to the great detective. But his connection with the stories was never quite as "exclusive" as Sidney Paget's had been. The *Strand* also

Left : George Hutchinson's illustration of Holmes's first meeting with Dr. John Watson. It appeared in the 1904 edition of *A Study in Scarlet.*

used Alfred Gilbert to illustrate Holmes extensively during this period. His illustrations have an intense realism that many readers greatly admired. But the honor of being the last artist to illustrate an original Holmes story went to Wiles. He created the images for the author's final three detective stories, including the very last, "Shoscombe Old Place."

In many ways, these illustrators fulfilled the function that was to be assumed by movie and television adaptations in the twentieth century, by fixing the image of Holmes in the collective imagination. Many of these screen versions were also heavily indebted to the original graphic artists, whose work inspired both their mise-en-scene and casting. Scenes from

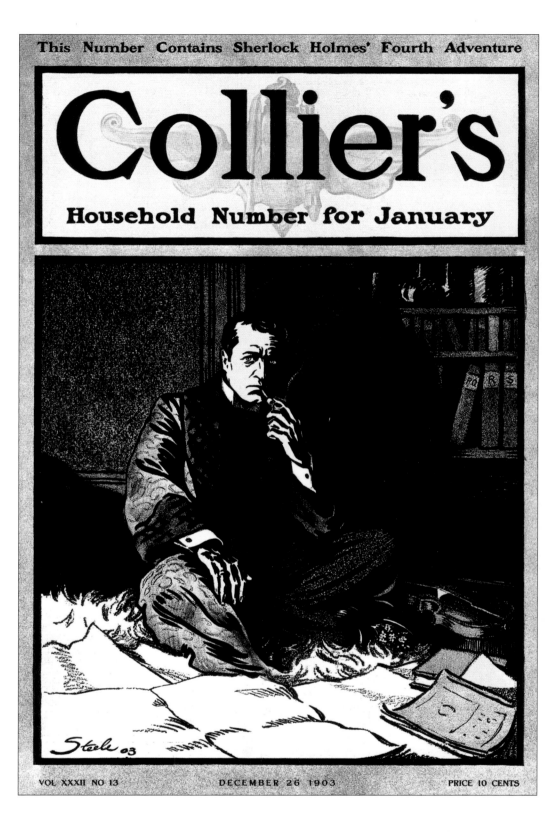

This Number Contains Sherlock Holmes' Fourth Adventure

Collier's

Household Number for January

Steele 03

VOL XXXII NO 13   DECEMBER 26 1903   PRICE 10 CENTS

Right: American illustrator Frederic Dorr Steele used the actor William Gillette as the model for his illustrations of Holmes. These appeared in *Colliers* magazine.

the famous Jeremy Brett Granada television series often look exactly like an animated version of Sidney Paget's work, and many actors who have played the role of Holmes have based their interpretations of the role on Paget and Steele's iconic portraits.

Sidney Paget has become a highly sought-after artist in his own right.

Above: J. Allen St. John produced this brilliant rendering of Holmes and Watson against a familiar London backdrop for the cover of the *Chicago Tribune* "Books" section of February 1949.

Above: Actor Jeremy Brett as Sherlock Holmes in the Granada Television series. He starred in forty-one episodes, produced between 1984 and 1994. The series truly recaptures the atmosphere of the original stories and is constantly rerun.

In 2004, his original drawing of Holmes and Moriarty, locked in mortal combat at the edge of the Reichenbach Falls, sold for $220,800 at Christie's New York.

Father of the Great Detective

Although Sherlock Holmes was not the first crime solver to appear in print, his appearance was fundamental in establishing the genre of detective fiction, one of the most successful literary forms ever.

Edgar Allan Poe's Monsieur C. Auguste Dupin is generally credited as being the world's first fictional detective, and Conan Doyle himself acknowledged his influence, describing him as "the best detective in fiction . . . [he] is unrivalled." Dupin first appeared in print in 1841 in a short story, "The Murders in the Rue Morgue," and many of the main ingredients of the genre of detective fiction were established in this single tale. But the inspiration behind this fictional character was almost certainly a real person, Eugene Francois Vidocq (1775–1857). Forger-turned-cop and first director of the Paris Surete Nationale, Vidocq had published a four-volume set of ghost-written *Memoires* (published in 1828 and 1829) that were very successful and widely read. Many consider him the "father of modern criminal investigation," as he was the first investigator to employ record keeping, criminology, and ballistics to solve his cases. Victor Hugo based two of his *Les Misérables* characters on Vidocq: Jean Valjean and Inspector Javert. Poe's fictional interpretation of the great detective was immediately successful, although Sherlock Holmes was dismissive of Dupin's detecting abilities. He describes him to Watson as a "very inferior fellow . . . He had some analytical genius, no doubt; but he was by no means such a phenomenon as Poe appeared to imagine."

Another fictional detective of whom Holmes speaks contemptuously is Monsieur Lecoq. Created by Emile Gaboriau, Lecoq was also based on the real life character of Vidocq, and appeared in five novels and a single short story between 1866 and 1876. Like Vidocq, he was "an old offender reconciled with the law." When Watson asks Holmes, "Does Lecoq come up to your idea of a detective?" Sherlock Holmes sniffs sardonically, "Lecoq was a miserable bungler." In reality, Conan Doyle's character eclipsed Lecoq, and stole his considerable following.

Several other first-rate authors of the Victorian period were quick to

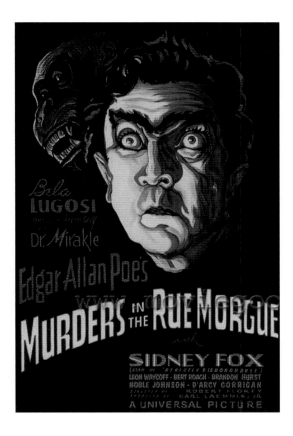

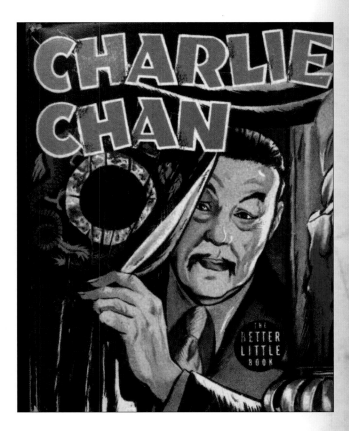

Above: Popular "pulp" versions of classic detective stories thrived from the 1920s onward.

spot the potential of this new genre, and to invent their own crime-busting heroes. Wilkie Collins created his famous Sergeant Cuff (*Woman in White*), while Charles Dickens offered his Inspector Bucket (*Bleak House*). British novelist Edmund Yates (1831-1894) ascribed the success of these books to their "creepy effect, as of pounded ice dropped down the back."

Conan Doyle can certainly be credited, not only with taking an existing literary form and ensuring its meteoric rise in popularity, but with adapting and extending the existing framework of the genre. Not only was he the first to create a series of stories around a single detective character, but he was also the first to endow his hero with a "modern" kind of intelligence and set of moral values that gave a new realism to his crime solving work. Sherlock's interest in chemistry and forensics is especially germane to this. But it is the fascinating character of Holmes himself that is Conan Doyle's most important contribution to the evolution of crime fiction. He is the progenitor of a long and distinguished dynasty of fictional detectives that continues to evolve to this day.

During Conan Doyle's lifetime, several contemporary authors tried to emulate his success, but their efforts were largely overshadowed by the popularity of Holmes. After his death, the first major fictional detective to gain the attention of the British public was G. K. Chesterton's *Father Brown*. Like Sherlock Holmes, Father Brown first appeared in the *Strand* in a series of short stories (fifty-one in total), which were then published in five compilations between 1911 and 1935. Unlike Holmes, Brown's methods of detection are intuitive rather than deductive. Chesterton went on to establish the British Detective Club for detective story writers.

Above: Charming period jackets for Raymond Chandler's novels. Chandler developed the "hardboiled" detective genre created by Dashiell Hammett. Author Mickey Spillane also wrote about a new breed of detective with flawed, rather than heroic personalities.

Members were obliged to swear an oath that their sleuths would not rely on "divine revelation, feminine intuition, mumbo-jumbo, jiggery-pokery, coincidence, or Act of God" to help solve their cases.

In Britain, the period between the wars became known as the Golden Age of detective story writing, and some of the greatest-ever fictional sleuths date from this time. These characters include Agatha Christie's Poirot, Dorothy L. Sayers's Lord Peter Wimsey, Margery Allingham's Albert Campion, and Ngaio Marsh's Roderick Alleyn. The success of the genre at this time in history may well have been due to its escapist nature. People in the post-war period were looking for healing and comfort; an ordered world where the guilty were punished and the innocent were vindicated was hugely attractive. In Britain, publishing forms were also changing, and full-length novels (often produced as paperbacks) took over the popular niche formerly occupied by serialized short stories.

On the other side of the Atlantic, the world of detective fiction was developing in an entirely different direction. Popular "pulp" detective story magazines were prevalent. *Black Mask* magazine was launched in 1921. It was to have a huge influence on the genre, for in 1923, the magazine published Dashiell Hammett's first detective story, "Arson Plus." The story featured a completely new kind of detective; a tough but chivalrous hero, hard enough to walk the mean streets, but "not himself mean." He was known simply as the Continental Op, and was the first recognizable member of the "hard-boiled school" of fictional American detectives. A world away from the "gentlemanly" work of contemporary British writers, hard-boiled became the "house style" of the American Golden Age of detective fiction. Several practitioners adopted Hammett's hard-boiled style, the most notable being Raymond Chandler. In 1939, Chandler introduced his brooding detective Philip Marlowe in the novel *The Big Sleep*. But this dark kind of detective story was not the only variety popular in post-war America. In 1925, Earl Derr Biggers introduced his inscrutable Oriental detective, Charlie Chan, in *The House Without a Key*. Chan was a completely unique, "benevolent, and philosophical" character, who was also to have a long and successful movie career.

Not all of the great detective writers who enjoyed Sherlock Holmes's legacy wrote in English. French-Belgian Georges Simeon created one of the world's best-known sleuths, Inspector Maigret, in 1931. The prolific Simeon wrote seventy-five Maigret novels and twenty-eight short stories about the detective, finishing in 1972. P. D. James accurately complimented Simeon as having "combined a high literary reputation with popular appeal."

After the Second World War, one of the first new American detective storywriters to be published was Mickey Spillane. Spillane introduced his famous hero, Mike Hammer, in his 1947 novel *I, The Jury*. Critically, his work moved the genre into a whole new area of gratuitous sex and violence, which provoked general outrage. But this did not hinder the great commercial success of Spillane's work, and he was far more interested in book sales than critical approval. Characteristically, he referred to his readers as "customers." He described his work as "garbage," but insisted that it was "good garbage."

Mike Hammer was the first of a completely new breed of American "detective," whose personalities were actually flawed, rather than merely eccentric, as in the endearing style of Holmes and many of his imitators. By contrast, sleuths of the British post-World War II generation were far more "decent," tending to be intellectual, sensitive, and burdened with high moral standards. This cultured coterie included Ruth Rendell's Inspector Reginald Wexford, P. D. James's Adam Dalgleish, and Colin Dexter's Inspector Morse.

From the 1970s onwards, another new trend was embraced by detective storywriters on both sides of the Atlantic: the female sleuth. British writer P. D. James introduced Cordelia Grey in 1972, while American writers Marcia Muller, Sue Grafton, and Sara Paretsky unveiled Sharon McCone, Kinsey Millhouse, and V. I. Warshawski, respectively.

By the 1980s and '90s, a new generation of male detectives had also come a long way since the strong silent type embodied by Holmes. This British archetype was usually brusque, often personally unsuccessful, but essentially right thinking. Examples include John Rebus by Ian Rankin, Charlie Resnick by John Harvey, and the duo of Dalziel and Pascoe by Reginald Hill. Perhaps the only famous exception to this troubled cast is Caroline Graham's Detective Chief Inspector Barnaby (the hero of her *Midsomer Murder* series), whose only serious personal problem is his wife's terrible cooking.

By stark contrast, contemporary American "detectives" are still often far more seriously damaged individuals. They struggle to overcome substance abuse and/or personal demons, while carrying the scars of each case on to their next investigation. This tortured crew includes James Lee Burke's Dave Robicheaux, Lawrence Block's Matt Scudder, and Michael Connelly's Harry Bosch.

Although modern detective "heroes" may seem to have moved a long way from the more obviously admirable nature of Holmes, it is interesting to note that the stories in which they appear still pivot around the character and the investigative skills of the hero detectives (with or without their Watsons), rather than the impersonal forensic technology of modern crime fighting. There is still an iconic place for the great detective in our culture, and it was the character of Sherlock Holmes that carved the cultural niche in which many others now stand.

The genre itself continues to gain popularity at every cultural level, from the essentially popular to the highly literary. Fiction bestseller lists continue to be crowded with wave after wave of imaginary crime fighters, while the best of the classic detective stories have lost none of their appeal and continue to be widely read and adapted for other media.

CHAPTER THREE

"The Air of London is sweeter for my presence."
SHERLOCK HOLMES

"London, that great cesspool into which all the loungers
and idlers of the Empire are irresistibly drained."
DR. JOHN WATSON, *"A STUDY IN SCARLET"*

"It is my belief, Watson, founded upon my experience, that the lowest
and vilest alleys of London do not present a more dreadful record
of sin than does the smiling and beautiful countryside."
SHERLOCK HOLMES

Sherlock Holmes in "The Great Wilderness"

BAKER STREET W1

CITY OF WESTMINSTER

Above: The Baker Street sign has a silhouette of its most famous resident in the top right hand corner.

Apart from the detecting duo themselves, "the great wilderness of London" is the most famous presence in the early Sherlock Holmes stories. Indeed, Holmes's encyclopedic knowledge of London is one of his greatest professional skills, facilitating the solution of many cases. In the minds of his readers, Sherlock's reputation became irrevocably interwoven with the streets of the British capital, and this close connection continues to fascinate. To this day, many tourists visit London with the intention of walking the streets the great detective walked and viewing the landmarks that Conan Doyle describes through Holmes's eyes. Many of the street names and places and interest with which Holmes was familiar have not only survived, but have remained almost unchanged for over a century: Pall Mall, the street where Mycroft Holmes has his club, The Diogenes; Simpson's on the Strand, where

Watson and Holmes dine; The British Museum where Holmes studies; Covent Garden Market where Holmes visits a dealer in geese; the railway stations at Charing Cross (from where Irene Adler escapes), Victoria, Waterloo, and Baker Street; Pope's Court, just off Fleet Street, where the Red-Headed League has its headquarters; Charing Cross Hospital, where Holmes is taken after the attack outside Piccadilly's Café Royal; Bow Street, where the man with a twisted lip begs; the theaters Holmes visits, the Haymarket, Lyceum, Covent Garden Opera House, and the Albert Hall (opened in 1871); the River Thames, where Holmes and Watson chase Jonathan Small in pursuit of the Agra Treasure; Lloyd's Bank in Pall Mall, where Watson keeps his deposit box, stuffed with un-recounted Holmes adventures. The upshot of this is that it is still perfectly possible to

Above: London's Fleet Street in the 1890s. The photograph instantly conveys what a crowded, bustling place London was at the time of the Holmes stories.

Above: A knife grinder. He is one of an army of street traders providing services to better-off Londoners.

Above Right: The familiar chimney sweep, complete with brushes, as characterized by Bert in *Mary Poppins*. At a time when coal fires were the only source of heat for millions of Londoners, sweeps were in constant demand.

Right: A Flower Girl offers her posies to a passer by. In reality this profession was often a "front" for an even older one!

walk in the great man's footsteps around the capital city.

When Holmes began his career as the world's first consulting detective in 1878, the great metropolis was exactly as Charles Dickens, Jr. catalogued it in *Dickens's Dictionary of London* (1879). The streets were filled with a revolving cavalcade of London characters, including street doctors, "nomades" (hawkers of cheap ornaments), ice-barrowmen, pickpockets, dustmen, costermongers, water-cart pushers, advertising board men, knife-grinders, chimney sweeps, chair-caners, apple women, flower girls, footpads, ginger-beer vendors, Italian street singers, shoeblacks, prostitutes, and crossing sweeps. But the human drama of this street life tended to belie the fact that London was starting to undergo a gradual but dramatic change, just beginning its evolution into a modern city.

As well as being the hub of the British Empire, London was a hugely important manufacturing and financial center that was powering its way to massive wealth. This wealth was to usher in great social change and create a vast new "middle" class. Despite this, the London poor continued to suffer grave social injustice, coping with extremely dangerous and unhealthy conditions in which to live and work. London's poorest areas were hotbeds of filth and vice, besmirched by "filthy cesspools and privies," putrefying garbage, and rotting dung-heaps. This vicious cocktail fouled the air and spread cholera and typhus, both of which were rife. On top of this, the industries in which the urban poor were employed often

Above: A market porter in front of London's Covent Garden Market.

Below: The barrel organ provided street entertainment and added to the roaring hubbub of the Victorian streets.

relied on fatally dangerous chemicals and processes and many workers were killed or disabled in the course of their labors.

Indeed, the poor were taken advantage of in every way imaginable. Virtually all the foodstuffs on which they relied were adulterated: bread with alum, milk with chalk and water, sausages with horsemeat, gin with vitriol, and sugar with Plaster of Paris. The very "butter" they were sold was actually lard colored with turmeric.

The social divide between London's rich and poor was immense. While the poor struggled to survive, the middle classes and gentry (like the Holmes family), enjoyed an increasingly civilized and sophisticated way of life. Elegance, etiquette, refined social interaction, and personal hygiene all became increasingly important during this period, and many luxuries and traditions that we still enjoy were introduced. Family photographs, days at the seaside, trips abroad, visits to (free entry) museums and art galleries, and restaurant meals all became a typical part of middle class life.

Above: As the middle classes became more affluent, luxuries like a day at the seaside, and a family photograph recording it, fell within reach for more people.

Right: Early gas lighting helped to stamp out crime in London. The lamps were individually tended to on a nightly basis.

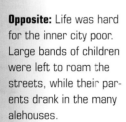

Opposite: Life was hard for the inner city poor. Large bands of children were left to roam the streets, while their parents drank in the many alehouses.

Right: Rich Victorians were less shielded from people of other classes than wealthy people are today. They interacted with the "lower" classes both in the streets and in their own homes (through the servants they employed).

Left: A group of female servants. They represent the thousands of working class Victorian women who lived "in service" to upper class families. This meant that the social classes mingled on a daily basis.

The first beginnings of a "modern" way of thinking also became apparent in the 1880s, just as Holmes and Watson were setting up home in Baker Street. Although British women were not to receive the vote until 1918, they did begin to enjoy more protection under the law. The Married Women's Property Act, for example, was passed in 1882, which meant that married women could now own property outright. The welfare of children and animals also became a cause for general disquiet and prosecutions mounted against the cruel and abusive. The writings of that other great Londoner, Charles Dickens, had greatly stimulated this concern for the unfortunate.

Many modern conveniences also became more widespread during this decade: running water, flushing lavatories, the omnibus, range stoves, steam trains, gaslight, typewriters, and early automobiles. Despite this, a comfortable middle class life relied on having domestic staff.

Some negative aspects of Victorian life were borne by every social class. Infant mortality continued to be extremely high and infectious diseases took victims from every social background, even the Royal family. During most summers, a great miasma of stench and filth hung over the capital and necessitated a general exodus to the country. Many Victorians were also locked into bitterly unhappy marriages (a regular theme in Holmes's cases and other literature of the period), as divorce continued to be almost impossible to obtain. An Act of Parliament was required to dissolve a marriage, which effectively limited this option to a very privileged few.

London itself was an enormous melting pot, where men and women of every social class were obliged to rub shoulders. In many ways, rich Victorians were less "shielded" from people of other classes than wealthy people are today. The legions of men and women that worked "in service" to middle and upper class families meant that the social classes met and mingled on a daily basis. They were interdependent, and the fabric of their lives became complexly interwoven.

The trio of Holmes, Watson, and Mrs. Hudson at Baker Street are a classic example of this mingling. Holmes is a member of the gentry, being the third son of an English country squire. His lack of interest in money

Left: The Underground railway was part of the rapidly growing public transport system in Victorian times. Cheaper travel greatly expanded the opportunity for working people to travel more widely. Public transport also led to the expansion of the London suburbs. The Underground network was particularly influential, allowing office workers to travel into the City much more quickly.

**221B BAKER STREET
LONDON NW1**

SHERLOCK HOLMES
CONSULTING DETECTIVE

Sherlock Holmes.

Above: The ethos of Sherlock Holmes's chosen profession of Consulting Detective was simple: "I listen to their story, they listen to my comments, I pocket my fee."

denotes a secure, though not necessarily lavish, background. But far from being men of leisure, he and his elder brother, Mycroft, must both earn their "bread and cheese." Evidently, Sherlock studied chemistry at university (probably Oxford or Cambridge, or both), so it is likely that Mycroft received a similar education to prepare him for the working world of the upper classes. Eventually, Mycroft Holmes becomes a senior civil servant, a classic career choice for sons of the gentry. The less conventional Sherlock invents his own profession, that of a "consulting detective," which he describes thus: "I listen to their story, they listen to my comments, I pocket my fee."

Watson's background is very similar to Conan Doyle's. He hails from the professional middle classes. Like Conan Doyle, Watson attends a minor public school (Wellington College in Hampshire) and studies medicine (entering London University in 1872, and working in surgery at St. Bartholemew's Hospital). After receiving his medical degree, he too travels abroad to practice his profession.

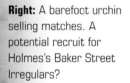

Right: A barefoot urchin selling matches. A potential recruit for Holmes's Baker Street Irregulars?

In 1878, Watson enrolls as an assistant surgeon in the British Army in India. But in 1880, he is wounded at the Battle of Maiwand, and is "demobbed" after contracting a life-threatening illness at the age of thirty-eight. At the time of his 1881 meeting with Holmes, Watson's only income is his army pension of eleven shillings and sixpence a day, but (like Conan Doyle) he later buys and sells several medical practices to provide himself with a living.

It is rather more difficult to determine Mrs. Hudson's social class. She

Below: The prospect of "nice rooms" in a genteel area, with a partner to share the expense, was an attractive proposition to Sherlock Holmes at the beginning of his career. The interior of 221b is recreated at the Sherlock Holmes Museum.

is not Holmes and Watson's housekeeper but their landlady, as it is she who owns the lease on 221B Baker Street (the Portman Estate was the freeholder, retaining ownership of the land on which the house is built). She is a businesswoman rather than a domestic servant (from the stories, we deduce that a cook and maid also live-in at 221B). Holmes and Watson confirm her higher status by referring to her as "Mrs. Hudson," rather than the more familiar "Hudson" they would use to address a servant. Despite this, Mrs. Hudson fulfills several housekeeper-like roles for her tenants. She "shows up" Holmes's more important clients to the sitting room. She also prepares coffee and at least some of their meals. (Holmes rudely describes her "cuisine" as being "a little limited.") She is probably a member of what would then have been referred to as the "lower middle classes." Despite their class differences, Mrs. Hudson's discreet presence becomes necessary to Holmes in particular and she is clearly devoted to him.

Above: During Queen Victoria's long reign, a comfortable domestic life became increasingly central to the British way of life.

Opposite: Elizabeth Chalmer's beautifully evocative watercolor of 221b Baker Street.

Through the Baker Street Irregulars (around a dozen street urchins recruited by Holmes to help him in his detective work), Holmes is also intimately connected with the rough life of the London streets. He refers to their leader, Wiggins, as his "dirty little lieutenant," and asserts that Wiggins's followers are his "eyes and ears on the streets." It is certainly true that his "Baker Street division of the detective police force" can get into places the great detective never could. But Holmes's unsentimental attitude to these children is quite illuminating. Although he pays them generously for their help and information, he does not seem to find their unescorted and un-parented state at all worrying or unacceptable. Quite the contrary, he appears to admire their independence and street-smart toughness.

Home Sweet Home

"Mid pleasures and palaces though we may roam,
Be it ever so humble, there's no place like home."
JOHN HOWARD PAYNE

"It was pleasant to Dr. Watson to find himself once more in the untidy room of the first floor in
Baker Street which had been the starting-point of so many remarkable adventures. He looked
round him at the scientific charts upon the wall, the acid-charred bench of chemicals, the violin-
case leaning in the corner, the coal scuttle, which continued of old the pipes and tobacco."
"THE ADVENTURE OF THE MAZARIN STONE"

During Queen Victoria's long reign (1837-1901), domestic life became increasingly central to the British way of life and a sentimental attachment to hearth and home, combined with the concept that "an Englishman's home is his castle," became a national credo. A massive house-building boom in the second half of the nineteenth century certainly made the goal of home ownership possible for many middle class families. But single gentlemen like our heroes usually preferred to live in lodgings where their housekeeping needs would be taken care of. Indeed, Holmes and Watson

Below: The presence of Madame Tussaud's famous "Wax-works exhibit and Chamber of Horrors" in the vicinity of Baker Street brought many pleasure seekers to the area.

meet through their mutual desire to inhabit comfortable, modestly priced lodgings. Watson is recovering from the enteric fever to which he fell victim in India, and needs a convivial home for his "shaken" nerves. Holmes also values the prospect of "nice rooms" and needs a tolerant partner to share the expense. When Holmes and Watson meet to view the apartment at 221B Baker Street, they immediately agree to rent the two "comfortable bedrooms and a single large airy sitting-room, cheerfully furnished and illuminated by two broad windows." The niceness of the rooms and the "moderate" nature of the rent are attractive to both parties.

At the time of their occupation (intermittently between 1881 and 1903), Baker Street was situated in Marylebone, a respectable area of London just north of the city center. The street partly overlooked the large open space of the Regents Park, which had been landscaped by John Nash in the early 1800s. The crescents and terraces that Nash built around the Park were some of the most fashionable addresses in London and they

Left and below: Baker Street Underground Station opened in 1863, so it would have been a useful transport link for residents of Baker Street during Holmes's residence.

The tiled walls of the "tube" station feature a ghostly silhouette of the famous detective. Baker Street station today is as busy as ever.

Above: 221b Baker Street today is the location of the Sherlock Holmes Museum, where Holmes's living rooms and paraphernalia are on display to visitors.

contained some of the city's most opulent residences. Slightly removed from the Park itself, Baker Street was not quite so fashionable or desirable. But throughout the eighteen century, it could claim a smattering of notable residents. These included William Pitt the Younger (Britain's youngest-ever Prime Minister), Edward Bulwer-Lytton (Member of Parliament and famous writer), The Right Hon. Henry Grattan (Irish parliamentarian), and Mrs. Sarah Siddons (the supremely famous tragic actress).

The character of the area was quite lively. Madame Tussaud's "Wax-work Exhibition and Chamber of Horrors" had been located at the Baker Street Bazaar since 1835 (admission, one shilling, Chamber of Horrors sixpence extra). The presence of the wax-works brought pleasure seekers of every kind into the area, and Baker Street itself became famous. Conveniently, the nearby Baker Street Station (one of the world's first underground stations) had been opened in 1863, built by the Metropolitan Railway Company. The modernized underground station commemorates the area's most famous resident with wall tiles featuring silhouettes of the great detective.

Most of the houses lining Baker Street were built in the late Georgian period. They were constructed as in terraces, in the highly symmetrical neo-classical style. Conan Doyle describes 221B as having four stories and being two window bays wide. As such, it would probably have been classified as a "third-rate" house, with an annual ground rent of between £150 and £350. Aristocratic families owned almost all the land that central London was built on and many followed the famous maxim of the fabulously wealthy Grosvenor family: "Always lease, never sell." This meant that vast family fortunes were founded on the ground rents of innumerable leaseholders like Mrs. Hudson.

The landlord of Marylebone was (and still is) the Portman Estate. In 1755, Portman (which had been established in the thirteenth century) leased land to a builder, a certain William Baker, upon which he laid out his eponymous thoroughfare.

This system of property ownership continues to announce itself on any street map of London. Whereas the highways and byways of many other cities are named for royals, political leaders, artists, scientists, and other notables, London streets testify to the influence of landlords, builders, and architects. The Duke of Westminster (head of the Grosvenor family), for example, owns London's American Embassy building, which is built on his property in Grosvenor Square. Portman Square, Street, Mews, Close, and Towers commemorate the freeholders of Marylebone.

From the beginning of the Holmes/Watson tenure at 221B, the apartment is the starting point for many of their adventures, and the layout and appearance of their "rooms" is gradually revealed through Conan Doyle's writing. Almost from the start, the apparent "reality" of the house (although 221B never actually existed), seemed to fascinate contemporary readers of the Sherlock Holmes stories. In response to this, the *Strand* published a floor plan of Watson and Holmes's second floor sitting room. It is immediately striking that the room served many different functions. Both men had their own desk (actually, Holmes seems to have two) and fireside chair (on either side of the bearskin rug). They share a dinner table. Holmes also has an "acid-charred" chemistry bench, while Watson lays claim to a large freestanding bookcase positioned between the windows. According to a Paget illustration for the *Naval Treaty*, the walls of the sitting room are lined with further bookshelves. Presumably, the pair share equal rights to the drinks table, pipe rack, and curtained recess. The *Strand* drawing also details a telephone. The famous lumber-room, a bathroom, and doors to the "two comfortable bedrooms" also appear on the plan.

Above: The official plaque commemorating Sherlock Holmes's occupancy of 221b Baker Street.

The second floor sitting room is where Sherlock indulges in his rather eccentric indoor target shooting, amid the "litter of pipes, tobacco-pouches, syringes, penknives, revolver-cartridges, and other debris." In a rather modern sounding complaint, Watson describes Holmes as "one of the most untidy men that ever drove a fellow-lodger to distraction."

The Holmes/Watson living quarters continue to exert the same allure they did to contemporary readers. This fascination has led to a number of recreations of the famous study and bedrooms. The most famous of these is undoubtedly the Sherlock Holmes Museum at 221B Baker Street, London NW1, the world's first museum dedicated to a fictional character. The house dates from 1815, and the correct number of steps (seventeen) lead up to the bachelors' apartment. Their rooms are recreated in meticulously authentic detail. In fact, nothing is displayed that is not mentioned in the stories, so the wonderful collection of Victoriana is highly evocative and authentic. The visitor feels that the famous duo may return to the beguilingly cozy sitting room at any moment, and that Mrs. Hudson will bring in the tea tray.

It is to this house that the volume of correspondence that is still addressed to the great detective is delivered. A full-time member of staff at the museum answers between forty and a hundred letters a week, most of which are requests for the detective's help. Sherlock also receives wedding invitations, birthday cards, and is invited to speaking engagements… Every year, several Christmas cards also arrive for Holmes, including one signed "John Watson."

THE SHERLOCK HOLMES MUSEUM

Pages 78 and 79: The Holmes's sitting room fireplace at the Sherlock Holmes Museum, and Paget's famous illustration of the same. They share the same restful and cozy ambience. Holmes's and Watson's hats rest on the table, together with the detective's pipe and magnifying glass. Holmes's Persian tobacco slipper can be seen on the mantle.

Page 80: The sitting room writing desk. The doorway leads to Holmes's bedroom.

Page 81: Mrs. Hudson has laid Holmes's and Watson's dining table with sparkling crystal and silver.

Page 82: The dressing table and storage cabinet in Holmes's bedroom. His deerstalker hat is on display, together with his actor's greasepaint, which he used to disguise himself. On the wall are pictures of the criminals he brought to justice.

Page 83: *Top:* The patriotic Holmes commemorated the Queen's initials, "V. R.," by firing a target pistol into the sitting room wall. *Bottom:* Holmes has left a book of violin music on his bedside table.

Page 85: Holmes's Spartan bedroom is pretty much as we would expect. Everything is clean and simple. His case of toiletries rests on the coverlet, and his suitcase is stowed underneath the bed. Everything seems ready for Holmes's departure to pursue a case.

CHAPTER FOUR

Medical and Forensic Science in the Sherlock Holmes Stories

· · · · · · · · · · · · · ·
·

Above: Fingerprints as a method of identifying criminals came into regular use during Holmes's career, and he was fully aware of this technique.

Medical and Forensic science both play an important role in the development of Holmes's character as a supremely rational, modern-minded investigator. The study of science and a passion for information also played a great role in Conan Doyle's intellectual life. Not only had he trained as a doctor himself, but he also retained a lively interest in the medical advances that were coming thick and fast in the nineteenth century. Conan Doyle had a great respect for the profession, which is very much reflected in his literary treatment of Holmes's "Boswell," the redoubtable Watson. A medical man through education and practice, he embodies all the best qualities of Victorian manhood: modest courage, steadfast loyalty, and discreet intelligence.

The medical profession underwent root and branch reform in the later part of the nineteenth century, particularly in the decades immediately preceding those covered by the Sherlockian canon. Medical practice was substantially professionalized and great advances in therapeutic treatment resulted in a much higher regard for its practitioners.

In 1846, surgical anesthesia had been introduced at Boston's Massachusetts General Hospital and this revolutionized the range of treatments that were then possible. Before anesthesia, surgery had been horribly barbaric. Attendants had to physically restrain writhing patients, and the surgeon's nerves often had to be braced with alcohol. All this meant that only very crude operations, such as amputations, were possible. But even though anesthesia facilitated far more delicate and wide-ranging surgical procedures, many patients continued to die from infection. Joseph Lister, Professor of Surgery at Edinburgh University (Conan Doyle's alma mater), pioneered antiseptic techniques in the 1870s, which resulted in far fewer postoperative deaths.

Before this scientific approach became prevalent, many doctors were little better than quacks, and their savage treatments (leaching, cold water dousing, cupping, blistering, and blood letting) led to them being regarded with fear and disdain. Many people preferred to rely on less aggressive home remedies that were no less effective. At this time, no formal qualifications were required to practice medicine, and physicians underwent an apprenticeship of approximately five years, rather than a formal education. Even the best of them were considered to be skilled tradesmen rather than professionals.

Below: Dr. Watson's medical bag, complete with his initials, J.H.W. (John Hamish Watson) is fully equipped with the medical equipment of the period.

Above: Joseph Lister pioneered the life-saving use of antiseptic surgery.

Complete lack of regulation meant that there was a huge range of ability and probity in the medical profession. Many highly dubious practices (which were either pointless or downright destructive) were commonplace in the "trade." Medical situations were often virtually hereditary; nepotism was rife. Also, apothecaries not only supplied drugs but prescribed and sold them. Many of their most common preparations were actually deadly rather than beneficial, and contained poisons such as arsenic and antimony. Only a very few medicines had any proven efficacy at all, and there was almost no medical research to test the validity of the drugs or treatments offered.

Dramatic change was afoot by the mid-eighteenth century. In Britain, the medical profession was completely reorganized into a three-tier structure of physicians, surgeons, and apothecaries. In 1858, Parliament passed the Medical Act to regulate unqualified practitioners, and the Medical Act Amendment of 1886 forbade unlicensed doctors to practice at all. The licensing system meant that medical training was upgraded to a university qualification. Several Universities responded by opening medical schools. This in turn led to a far greater number of students wishing to enter the medical profession, as it was now considered suitable for "gentlemen."

Pharmacy was subjected to far tighter regulations as well. A list of approved drugs, the National Pharmacopoeia, was instigated in 1864 and it became illegal to prescribe any drugs that did not appear on this register.

By 1848, Edinburgh University had gained a reputation both for giving the country's most thorough medical training, and for its progressive attitudes. The University pioneered the entry of women into the medical profession and admitted its first female medic, Sophia Jex Blake, in 1869. Conan Doyle enrolled a few years later, in 1876, by which time Scottish and European universities graduated around thirty percent of British doctors.

By the 1880s, Edinburgh's direct competitor, the London University Medical School, was best known for its extremely demanding final examination. The school graduated thirty-two percent of all British physicians, including James Watson (class of 1878). Sherlock Holmes was a post-graduate student at London University, studying chemistry and anatomy. London was also famous for its high standards of nursing (Elizabeth Fry's Nursing Sisters was founded in 1840), for the eminence of its surgeons (including the Royal Surgeon Sir James Paget), and for its high standards of antiseptic cleanliness. Oxford and Cambridge, on the other hand, prided themselves on the rather less practical atmosphere of "scientific culture" that they offered their students. It is thought that Sherlock Holmes studied his undergraduate degree in chemistry at either one, or both, of these venerable institutions.

The extremely high standards set by London University at this time are particularly interesting to readers of the canon. Watson entered the University's medical school in 1872 and graduated from it in 1878.

London's rigorous training, and the arduous nature of its medical examination, would have been well understood by Conan Doyle. This is a clear indicator that he considered Watson to be a highly intelligent and capable man, far from the buffoonish character often portrayed in screen adaptations of the novels. It seems to have been forgotten by some interpreters of the role that Watson is not only Holmes's highly regarded friend but also his chronicler. He is only less intelligent than Holmes in the way that every "normal" person is inferior to a genius. In passing, these cartoonish "Watsons" are also often far too elderly and grizzled. Watson is only thirty-eight when he first meets Holmes in 1881, just two years older than the great detective, and seven years older than Conan Doyle. Watson succeeds in having a successful "combined" career in writing and medicine, just as Conan Doyle may have hoped to balance.

The radical changes to the medical profession made it far more

Overleaf: Holmes's chemical bench at the Sherlock Holmes Museum and Sidney Paget's rendering of Holmes at work in his illustration for *The Adventure of the Naval Treaty.*
Below: A Victorian surgeon's chest, which grotesquely resembles a carpenter's tool kit. Surgery was generally restricted to amputation or trepanning, and many died from infection or shock before the introduction of antiseptics and anesthetic.

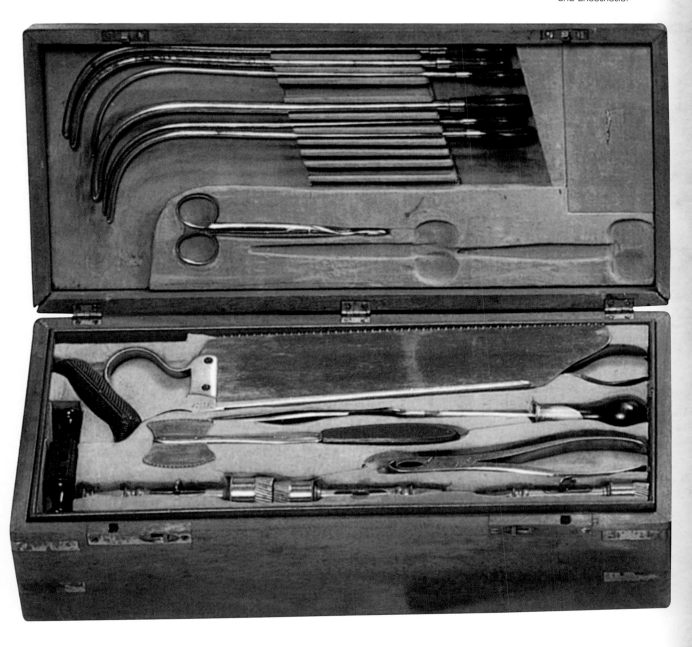

"HOLMES WAS WORKING HARD OVER A CHEMICAL INVESTIGATION."

attractive to a higher caliber individual and to men from higher social classes. (At this time, most women in medicine continued to be either nurses or midwives.) Able and intelligent men (like Watson and Conan Doyle) were attracted to the profession by the high status that doctors now enjoyed, and the possibility of contributing to further scientific advances. The prospect of a good living must also have been appealing. At the top of his profession, a thriving London consultant could earn as much as £4,000 or £5,000 a year and enjoy a lavish lifestyle of country houses, carriages, and servants. Perhaps Conan Doyle was hoping for this kind of success when he moved to Upper Wimpole Street to practice ophthalmology. In choosing to specialize, Conan Doyle was reflecting the trend in European medical practice, where doctors tended to focus on specific conditions (including obstetrics and lunacy) or parts of the body. In 1891, he had traveled to both Vienna and Paris to study his chosen field. But perhaps his lack of success reflected the British patient's preference for a more holistic approach from doctors in "general" practice. Watson certainly follows this course, and though his professional aspirations may be modest, he succeeds in supporting his family, just as his creator had done.

Both Conan Doyle and Watson were also able to use their medical skills to travel abroad. At this time, the British Empire was expanding rapidly, and doctors were needed to support explorers, traders, and the army itself. Only with their professional assistance could the British continue to extend their far-flung influence.

Having matriculated as a doctor in 1881, Conan Doyle gave up practicing just a decade later, in 1891. His great success as a writer had completely outshone his limited achievements in the medical profession, and perhaps the "suspicious" death of John Hawkins so early in his career, had eroded some of his professional self-confidence. But Conan Doyle maintained a strong interest in medical science throughout his life, particularly in forensic medicine. More importantly, his knowledge of the subject was to become intrinsic to his most successful work.

Conan Doyle's alma mater, Edinburgh University, was a pioneering force in the study of forensic medicine, and had had a "chair" in the subject since 1807. Conan Doyle would certainly have known the work of Sir Robert Christison, Edinburgh's Professor of Forensic Medicine between 1822 and 1832. During his tenure, Christison published his *Treatise on Poisons* (1829), and this was to become the standard English-language work on toxicology. Conan Doyle's university mentor, Dr. Joseph Bell, is also credited as a pioneer of forensic science and was famous for his use of acute observation to make medical diagnoses. Bell's methodology and academic knowledge forms at least an element of Holmes's character, in which a "profound" understanding of chemistry, anatomy, and toxicology are combined. Conan Doyle's character announces himself as an expert in these fields in his very first meeting with Watson. He refers to the discovery of "hemoglobin . . . the most

Opposite: tDr. Watson's bedroom at the Sherlock Holmes Museum displays his collected medical journals and copies of *The Lancet,* together with an early device for measuring blood pressure, and a fully stocked medical cabinet.

Right: A portable medical kit, which belonged to Dr. F.L. Miner. It contains many popular drugs of the nineteenth century, including chloral hydrate, chloroform, and potassium bromide.

practical medico-legal discovery for years . . . it gives us an infallible test for blood stains." In fact, the German scientist Christian Friedrich Schonbein had developed a test to detect hemoglobin in 1865.

Conan Doyle had also read Edgar Allan Poe's "The Murders in the Rue Morgue" (1841) and saw how Vidocq's real life "heirs" in the Parisian police force used both forensic science and the study of criminology. In fact, it was in Poe's "The Mystery of Marie Roget" that the first fictional crime was to be solved by forensic evidence found on the victim's body. This use of forensics in both fictional and real-life crime solving undoubtedly inspired Conan Doyle's creation of Holmes. But through his character, Conan Doyle develops this theme much further. In doing so, he effectively captured the zeitgeist of Victorian England. The great advances in technology fascinated his contemporaries and the detective story

Above: Police methods left a lot to be desired. Bodies were quickly removed from crime scenes to avoid public unrest. This was often before a proper forensic examination had been carried out. This kind of poor forensic practice was to become a seriously negative factor in the search for Jack the Ripper, who was never brought to justice.

proved a great medium to explore popular science. This led to such prominent figures as novelist Henry James (1843–1916), being rather dismissive of the genre, describing it as "not so much a work of art as a work of science." But Conan Doyle's brilliant blend of imagination and forensic fact is the double helix at the heart of Holmes's success.

The nineteenth century saw an explosion of major forensic breakthroughs, especially during its later decades, the period in which Holmes's cases are set. Conan Doyle was fully aware of these discoveries and shared his knowledge with the great detective. Many of these forensic techniques remain in daily use by crime scene investigators.

The fundamental precept of forensic science was laid down by criminologist Locard in L'enquelle Criminelle et les Methodes Scientifique (1904), in which he stated, "Every contact leaves a trace." A whole raft of nineteenth- and early twentieth-century forensic work justified Locard's assertion:

☛ In 1813, Mathiau Bonaventure Orfila was the first pathologist to use a microscope to examine blood and semen at crime scenes.

☛ In 1835, Henry Goddard (one of Scotland Yard's original Bow Street Runners) was the first person to use a system of bullet comparison to investigate a crime.

☛ James Marsh developed his "Marsh Test" in 1836, to detect the presence of arsenic in human tissue.

☛ Alfred Swaine Taylor and Samuel Wilks's classic work of the 1860s made it possible to determine time of death by measuring the fall in body temperature. They achieved this by placing the exposed bulb of a thermometer on the skin of the cadaver's abdomen.

☛ Dr. Henry Faulks was the first person to realize the importance of fingerprints at a crime scene. Sir Francis Galton formalized this theory in his book *Fingerprints* (1892) and identified how individual prints could be recognized. "Galton's Details" are still in use today. Galton's work led the Head of Scotland Yard, Sir Edward Richard Henry, to replace anthropometrics with fingerprints as the force's main source of biometric information.

Below: A pestle and mortar would have been used to grind residues into a powder for forensic tests.

☛ In 1893, Austrian magistrate Hans Gross published his Manual for Examining Magistrates. In essence, this was a handbook of forensic investigation for legal professionals. Although Gross never read the Holmes stories, his work is remarkably "Holmesian" in its sophistication.

☛ In the early 1900s, Georg Popp established the precepts of forensic geology. This was rather later than Holmes's manifest interest in the subject. Watson tells us how, in the 1880s, Holmes could tell "at a glance different soils from each other."

Before these advances in forensic science, the only evidence available to the police was circumstantial. Inevitably, this had resulted in terrible miscarriages of justice. By using a combination of formidable observational powers and deep scientific knowledge, Holmes becomes the "seeker after hidden truth, the fathomer of mysteries, the hound of justice upon the trail of injustice and official apathy." He is the paradigm of a ruthless investigator.

Through his own experiments, and voracious reading, Holmes had become expert in a wide spectrum of physical

Below: Tests proved that the stains on this rolling pin were blood, and it was used as an unconventional murder weapon. Schonbein had developed a test for hemoglobin in 1863.

evidence, including tracks, tobacco ashes, human remains, body fluids, gunpowder residue, and poisons (including belladonna, arsenic, and opium). He also has an up-to-date knowledge of forensics, which is featured in many canon stories. The "well-marked print of a thumb" on a whitewashed wall in "The Adventure of the Norwood Builder" and the trajectory and impact of a bullet in the "Reigate Squires" are just two examples. Holmes's investigative career was built on his early training as a chemist and he exhibits a deep understanding of the subject throughout his career. He immediately recognizes the smell of both iodoform, the "pleasantly almondy odor" of prussic acid, and instantly distinguishes the black marks left by silver nitrate. Holmes is also an early exponent of handwriting analysis. In The *Hound of the Baskervilles*, the great detective describes it as "my special hobby."

Always anxious to be well-informed and *au fait* with the latest scientific discoveries, Conan Doyle did not only use his understanding of forensic science in his fictional work but brought it to bear on real-life cases. Lady Conan Doyle described how he solved several mysteries that had completely baffled the police, and she told how "He was able, through his remarkable power of deduction and intelligence to locate missing people whose relatives had given them up as lost or murdered." But once again, the creator was eclipsed by his creation. Holmes's ability as a chemist was so highly regarded that the Royal Society of Chemistry awarded him a "posthumous" Honorary Fellowship.

Both Conan Doyle and his character have made their own contribution to the study of criminology. So successful was the author's search for realism that the Sherlockian cases are used as exemplars by professors of forensic medicine the world over. Conan Doyle's contemporary, French forensics expert Edmund Locard, may have been the first to realize the potential of his work when he advised his students to familiarize themselves with Sherlock Holmes's cases. As well as being the inventor of the "silent witness" axiom, that "Every contact leaves a trace,"

Above: Both bloodstains and fingerprints identified this meat cleaver as another murder weapon.

Above: The well-defined bloody thumbprint on a whitewashed wall helped to solve the case of "The Norwood Builder."

Locard also established the "Exchange Principal," that stated that when a criminal comes into contact with a victim, they not only leave evidence at the scene of the crime but also take evidence away with them. Locard realized that the Holmes stories illustrated both of these principles. In fact, Conan Doyle's work effectively began a practice of public education, showing how crimes can be solved with the intelligent interpretation of evidence. This precept features in much modern crime fiction, with *CSI* the ultimate contemporary example.

The "forensic" literary legacy left by Conan Doyle and Sherlock Holmes is highly significant. Not only did the Holmes stories popularize the genre of detective fiction, but their accuracy also led to a tradition of extreme realism that continues to this day. Dame Agatha Christie, for example, used her experience as a trained chemist to great effect in her novels, and it is interesting to note that two of the most successful modern practitioners of crime fiction, Katy Reich and Patricia Cornwell, are both forensic professionals. (Reich is a forensic anthropologist, and Cornwell was a clerk in a forensic pathologist's office.) Their work, like that of Conan Doyle, defies Henry James's criticism by achieving a true marriage of art and science.

But many believe that Holmes's methods have also had a wider

Left: The Black Museum at Scotland Yard has been a repository for crime scene evidence since the early days of crime detection. It is closed to public access and serves as a training facility for the Metropolitan Police Force.

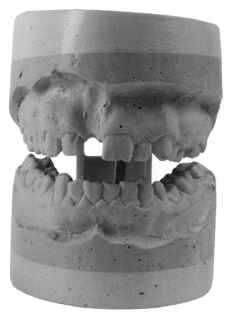

Left: This harrowing forensic specimen from the Kent Police Museum demonstrates the use of plaster casts and dental evidence in criminal identification. The pattern of the teeth exactly matches the dreadful wound on the victim's body.

influence on the world of real life crime fighting. When he traveled to London in 1912, America's greatest living detective, William J. Burns met with Conan Doyle, and assured him that Sherlock Holmes's methodology was entirely practical. Burns later maintained that Holmes's popularity actually influenced the science of criminal detection towards the use of more scientific methods, and that his cases popularized forensics and pathology. Perhaps this is the sleuth's greatest, living, legacy.

CHAPTER FIVE

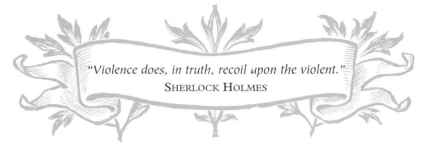

"Violence does, in truth, recoil upon the violent."
SHERLOCK HOLMES

Sherlock Holmes and the Law

Above: A sergeant in the Victorian police force. After 1869, beards were encouraged.

Crime, detection, and punishment were huge issues during Sherlock Holmes's professional era. It was a time when some of the most celebrated and terrible crimes ever committed were perpetrated. The expediential growth of London in particular led to a tidal wave of criminality, thriving on poverty, vagrancy, and degradation. Although the motives in Holmes's cases tend to be far more intellectual and sophisticated, many of the crimes he investigates in the canon have as strong an element of brutality as contemporary "real life" crimes. In the early part of his career at least, the agencies of law enforcement were still in their infancy. But over the course of his casework, their move towards a far higher degree of organisation and professionalism was significant.

As well as the professionalism of the police force, techniques of criminal deduction were also developing during this period. Not only were many discoveries made to advance the use of forensic science in solving crime, but the police service itself was also completely reorganized, as were the judicial and penal systems.

Holmes and Scotland Yard

Throughout his career, Holmes is often portrayed as working in parallel

with various "Inspectors" from Scotland Yard. They are usually at least one pace behind the Great Detective, but are often credited with his successes. Scotland Yard was (and is) the headquarters of London's Metropolitan Police Service, and was founded in 1829. The organization was named after its original location in Great Scotland Yard, but was moved to new premises on London's Victorian Embankment in 1890, overlooking the River Thames. Holmes's respect for Scotland Yard is not high, Watson describes how the confidence that the popular press has in the crime solving ability of the organisation affords him "considerable amusement." But his scorn is probably directed at the Yard's rather elementary and "conventional" methods of detection, rather than the calibre of its officers. Forensic science would certainly have been more familiar to Holmes than to his colleagues in the police force. Indeed, it was not until 1879 that the Metropolitan police force gave its officers a basic framework of crime scene etiquette, so that "a body must not be moved… and the public must not be admitted (to the room)."

Several "Yard" officers, together with a couple of Inspectors from provincial police forces, make an appearance in the Sherlock Holmes's stories. These men are named as Inspectors G. Lestrade, Tobias Gregson, Baynes, Bradstreet, Stanley Hopkins, Athelney-Jones, MacDonald, Martin, and Youghal. In his self-created role as the world's only "unofficial consulting detective," Holmes often collaborates with the police, pronouncing a "specialist's opinion" when "Gregson or Lestrade or

Above: Great Scotland Yard, the original headquarters of the Metropolitan Police.

Above: Scotland Yard's premises in the 1890s.

Above: Holmes admired Allan Pinkerton for his methods of detection.

Athelney Jones are out of their depth."

Interestingly, Leverton, a Pinkerton detective also makes his appearance in the canon, in "*The Adventure of the Red Circle.*" The American is described as a "quiet, businesslike young man," and is already known to Holmes as the "hero of the Long Island cave Mystery." Allan Pinkerton had founded his National Detective Agency in Chicago in 1850, and like Holmes, was famous for his "great power of observation and courage." Forerunner of the FBI, the Pinkerton Agency spearheaded the use of forensic and ballistic evidence, "stings," and intelligence gathering; all techniques found in Holmes's armory.

Inspector Lestrade is the police office who appears most often in the canon. He is locked in professional rivalry with his fellow detective, Tobias Gregson, and Holmes describes the two officers as being "as jealous as a pair of professional beauties." Both are introduced to in Holmes's very first case, "*A Study in Scarlet.*" The pair is also familiar to the public, and described as "well-known officers" in a fictional edition of *The London Standard.* Holmes refers to Lestrade as "the best of the professionals, I think," meaning that he is the most able man employed by Scotland Yard. Although Holmes also describes Lestrade as being "devoid of reason," he obviously admires Lestrade's grit

Left: Inspector Lestrade of Scotland Yard demonstrates his bulldog spirit in *A Study In Scarlet*.

and determination; believing him to be as "tenacious as a bull dog." The regard was mutual. Although Lestrade is often exasperated by Holmes's unconventional methods, he confesses his great regard for Holmes in "*The Six Napoleons*". "We're not jealous of you down at Scotland Yard, no sir, we are damned proud of you." Holmes is visibly moved by this generous compliment from a fellow professional.

Lestrade's rival, "the fair-haired" Inspector Tobias Gregson is also a regular canon character, and (like Lestrade), he also solicits Holmes's assistance in difficult cases. Holmes believes him to be the more intelligent of the two, and refers to him as "the smartest of the Scotland Yarders. He and Lestrade are the pick of a bad lot." Gregson also makes an impression on Watson, who describes the cool and ruthless way in which he works.

Rather than use the traditional methodology of Scotland Yard, the young Inspector Stanley Hopkins attempts to employ Holmes's own deductive techniques in his own investigations. He also refers several cases to his

Left: Lestrade presents a doubtful Holmes with his interpretation of the evidence in the case of "The Norwood Builder."

Below: Provincial policemen with the Inspector standing. Holmes encounters the provincial police in many of his cases and displays little regard for them, with the notable exception of Inspector Baynes of the Surrey Constabulary. Holmes encounters Baynes in "The Adventure of Wisteria Lodge."

mentor, including "*The Adventure of Black Peter*" and "*The Adventure of the Abbey Grange.*" Although the Great Detective is critical of Hopkins's application of his methods, he nevertheless "has high hopes for his career."

Ironically, the only police detective who ever seriously challenges Holmes's ability, and wins his unequivocal regard, does not work in London at all. Inspector Baynes belongs to the provincial police force of "leafy" Surrey, the county that Conan Doyle was to make his home. In "*The Adventure of Wisteria Lodge*" the two men work with different methods, ("We all have our little ways. You try yours and I will try mine") but are both simultaneously on the trail of Henderson/Murillo, and reach the denouement together. Holmes is genuinely impressed by Baynes's ability, he "laid his hand upon the inspector's shoulder. "You will rise high you in your profession. You have instinct and intuition." This remark is highly revealing. It completely refutes the often-held idea that Holmes's believed only cool reason and intellectual ability were required to solve crimes. In fact, he considers intuition an imperative part of a detective's equipment.

Good career prospects attracted many able men, like Gregson and Lestrade, to join the Metropolitan Police, which is generally considered to

Above: Early examples of "bobbies on bicycles." Note the forage caps.

Below: Before the issue of the traditional domed helmet, Victorian policemen wore kepis.

Above: Joining the police force was considered a prestigious career opportunity, and recruitment standards became increasingly high.

have been the first modern police service. To join, a man needed to be less than 35 years of age, at least 5 feet 7 inches tall, literate, and of good character. Police recruits were drawn from a variety of backgrounds. A survey of 1874 revealed that thirty-one per cent came from agricultural jobs, twelve per cent from a military background, five per from other police forces, but the majority were drawn from general laboring jobs. The majority of these recruits came from outside London, including 2.5% from Scotland, and 6.5% from Ireland.

Once a man had been accepted, the Metropolitan police force's policy of merit-based internal promotion meant that he had every chance to improve his prospects. The career path of Metropolitan officer Donald Swanson, who was appointed to head the Jack the Ripper enquiry in August 1888, gives us a good idea of what a high-flying police officer could achieve. Born in Wick, Scotland, Swanson enrolled in the Metropolitan police force in 1868 at the (usual) age of twenty. His warrant card number was 50282. In 1882, he achieved the rank of Inspector, and was promoted to Chief Inspector in the Criminal Investigation Department in 1887. In 1896, he became the Superintendent of Scotland Yard, and retired in 1906 at the age of fifty-eight. The Metropolitan's system of internal promotion to higher rank meant that able officers, like Lestrade and Gregson, were able to achieve improved pay and working

Right: The idea of the policeman on his beat was a sound one. Visible policing in Victorian times nipped many crimes in the bud.

Above: Before the organization of the modern police force, Britain relied on night watchman like this one. They were usually older men, possibly with military experience. They were equipped with a lantern, and a cutlass or truncheon.

Left: An early police officer pictured with the tools of his trade: handcuffs, truncheon, frock coat, top hat, duty band, and collar serial number.

conditions, greater authority, and prestige. From his career timetable, it would seem safe to assume that Lestrade, Gregson, and the other "Inspectors" of the canon are likely to be in their thirties.

Over the course of Swanson's career, the "Met" grew rapidly. In 1884, the force consisted of 13,319 officers, which included 1,383 working the "beat." The force had grown to 14,106 officers in 1888. The Metropolitan police was divided into several divisions. A Superintendent, each of whom had four inspectors and sixteen sergeants, headed each division.

The Metropolitan force had been created in 1829, when Parliament passed the Metropolitan Police Act. It was an attempt to formalize law enforcement in the capital, and superseded the ancient practice of "The Watch," where a body of privately employed men patrolled the streets at night. Social and economic change meant that people flooded into Britain's cities, and the informal policing arrangements dating from the Middle Ages were completely ineffective, and the streets became increasingly unsafe. Shocked by this state of affairs, the law-abiding public demanded proper protection.

Police Equipment

Their equipment was basic to say the least, just a truncheon (made from gutta percha), a wooden rattle to summon help, and a lamp. A few years later, a whistle was substituted for the rattle. The early uniform was replaced with the more familiar tunic and helmet in 1860.

Left: A police pacifier made of hard tropical wood.

Below: A Tipstaff, a constable's original badge of office.

Below and above: Two beat officers' truncheons made from hardwood.

Above: Many nineteenth century "pacifiers" were ornately decorated with the coat of arms of the county from which the police force was drawn.

Above: A one-candle power police lamp.

Right: A police rattle. This was used to attract attention and summon help.

Right: The oil powered bull's-eye lamp replaced the candle lamp.

Left: The police whistle was a replacement for the rattle, shown above.

Right: A detail of the Victorian police belt. Each county force had its coat of arms cast into the buckle.

Above: The duty band. This was worn as a belt and signified that the wearer was on duty.

Above: The Victorian constable in full uniform. He wears a blue tunic with matching trousers, a leather belt, black boots, and a helmet with a chinstrap.

Above: The classic style British policeman's helmet was first introduced in 1863.

Originally, Robert Peel's legislation created eight police divisions. These first policemen were equipped with a civilian-style blue uniform, consisting of a reinforced top ("pot") hat and frock coat and trousers, and white gloves. Each constable also had his number embroidered on his shoulder. Policemen were also expected to be clean-shaven at this time, though this rule was relaxed in 1869. Their equipment was basic to say the least, just a truncheon (made from gutta percha), a wooden rattle to summon help, and a lamp. A few years later, a whistle was substituted for the rattle. The early uniform was replaced with the more familiar tunic and helmet in 1860. Over 51% of the first recruits to the police force were dismissed quite quickly, the vast majority for being drunk on duty. But the great challenge facing the new force began apparent all too quickly, when PC Joseph Grantham became the first serving officer to be killed on duty in 1829.

At this stage, the force consisted of around 3,300 men, but a period of rioting exposed the thinness of their ranks, and more officers were recruited. 5,493 were in place by

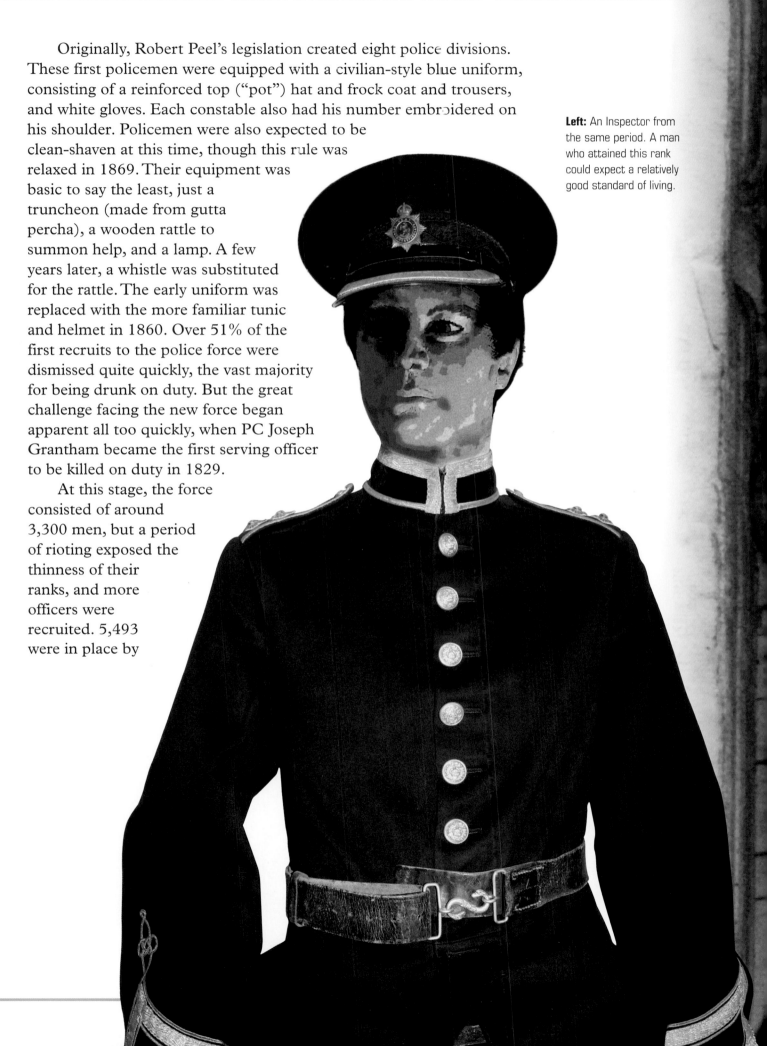

Left: An Inspector from the same period. A man who attained this rank could expect a relatively good standard of living.

Left: A mounted police officer's cutlass. Swords of this type were still used in action.

Above: The mounted policeman was (and remains) an important resource in riot control. There was a high level of political unrest in Victorian times.

Below: A mounted policeman's belt and pouch, displaying the Kent County coat of arms.

1849. A ratio of one police officer to every 450 citizens was considered ideal, but this was not achieved until later in the century. Other famous London crime fighting institutions, such as the Bow Street Runners were also absorbed into the "Met," and the area covered by the force was gradually increased to include the outlying districts of the capital. Eighteen divisions now policed 688 square miles of some of the most crime-ridden streets in the world. Crime was also escalating at a frightening pace. In 1846, 14,091 robberies were reported, including 60 stolen dogs. The clear up rate was rather less impressive. Only 4,551 criminals were convicted and sentenced in that year, while magistrates acquitted 31,572 defendants.

Crime and Punishment

Corruption and lack of legal knowledge were rife amongst the judiciary, even at the Old Bailey, where the most serious crimes in Britain (including treason, murder, forgery, and burglary) were tried. Defendants were not even entitled to legal representation unless they could afford to pay for it. There was also a serious lack of consistency in sentencing, as this was usually done by different court to the one that had found the

Left: London's Old Bailey was the highest court in the land. The present building dates from 1902 and was built on the site of the infamous Newgate Prison. The statue on the top of the dome is of Lady Justice who holds a sword in her right hand as a symbol of the power to punish, and a set of scales in her left symbolizing the power of equity

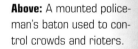

Above: A mounted policeman's baton used to control crowds and rioters.

Above: Ex –policeman James Berry was the official hangman for eight years between 1884 and 1892. His position gained him a macabre celebrity.

Above: Charles Dickens wrote about the severity of the legal system in his novels.

Below: Magwich the convict attacks Pip in the graveyard on the Cooling Marshes in Dickens's *Great Expectations*.

defendant guilty. Error was hardly ever on the side of leniency, and young men in particular were often hung for trivial crimes including petty theft. In effect, many commentators viewed the judicial system as an instrument of social control. Hanging was only limited to perpetrators of murder and treason in 1861.

For criminals sentenced to custodial sentences, prison conditions were dreadful. As author Charles Dickens wrote, "At the time, jails were much neglected." Most prisoners were obliged to pay for their food and lodging, and the sight of prisoners begging from visitors was commonplace. They were also obliged to pay a release tariff at the end of their sentence. If they had no means of raising the money, they were simply left in goal.

In fact, Charles Dickens had received an all-too-intimate glimpse of the prison system at the age of twelve, when his father spent three months in the Marshalsea debtors' prison. As was usual, the entire family was forced to join him there,

"I've been done everything to, pretty well — except hanged. I've been locked up . . . (and) carted here and carted there. . . stuck in stocks, and whipped and worried and drove."

MAGWITCH, DICKEN'S *Great Expectations*

Right: The infamous Newgate jail where public executions were popular spectacles until the 1860s.

Below: A Victorian prison warder holds a cell door open.

although the unfortunate Charles was sent to work in a shoe-blacking factory during the day. His brush with the wrong side of the law gave him a lifelong obsession with prison and the British legal system, and they appear in all his major novels. But it is his sympathetic biography of the convict Abel Magwitch in *Great Expectations* that gives us perhaps his most extraordinary insight into the English criminal justice system in the mid-nineteenth century. Its insight into the criminal mind is extraordinarily sympathetic for the time in which it was written (between 1852 and 1853). Caught stealing turnips as a child, Magwitch spends his entire life "In jail and out of jail, in jail and out of jail, in jail and out of jail," for increasingly vicious crimes. In effect, he becomes a victim of a brutal system designed to punish rather than rehabilitate: "I've been done everything to, pretty well – except hanged. I've been locked up ... (and) carted here and carted there... stuck in stocks, and whipped and worried and drove." Britain finally turns his back on Magwitch altogether, and he is transported to the penal colony in New South Wales, Australia. (This practice was reserved for only the most serious criminals in 1853.) Returning to England, he only misses being

Above: The inside of a preserved police cell. An iron latch runs across the inspection hatch of its solid door.

Left: Once inside, a wooden tray was the only concession to comfort.

Right: The Victorian period saw extensive rioting and the mounted police were often deployed.

Above and opposite: The birch was used as a means of punishment until the 1950s. Scenes like this flogging at Newgate Prison were commonplace.

hung by dying of natural causes. Dickens shows how despite his dreadful life, Magwitch has a spark of true goodness, and suggests that more humane treatment could have fostered, rather than extinguished this. As his fame and influence grew, Dickens became heavily involved in the movement to reform British prisons, and travelled to America examine the various penitentiary systems prevalent at the time.

As well as prison, convicts could be subjected to a fearful range of capital and corporal punishments. Flogging was commonplace, and boys as young as eight were hung right up until the 1850s. Public executions persisted until 1868, and even heavily pregnant women were not spared. A good view at London's Newgate hanging ground was a highly desirable commodity, and could change hands for as much as ten pounds.

By the end of the century, the prison system had changed dramatically. In place of filth, starvation, and degradation, the prisons were models of a new kind of equally oppressive regime. In the "silent

Flogging was commonplace, and boys as young as eight were hung right up until the 1850s.

Below: Leg irons were used to restrain prisoners in Victorian times.

Above and left: Two examples of handcuffs, or "Darbys" as they were known. These are from the collection of the Kent Police Museum. Every police constable would carry a pair.

Left: City Road Police station in the late nineteenth century. It was one of several large, inner city police stations built to control crime. Four officers stand proudly in the front portal.

Above: The Scales of Justice stone tablet, which appears on the wall of the building.

Right: The imposing portal of Bow Street police station complete with its ornate metal lamps, which were white instead of the usual blue reportedly at the request of Queen Victoria, who used to visit the nearby Royal Opera House.

A famous name in crime detection in London, Bow Street was the home of the original Bow Street Runners. This body of men was eventually absorbed into the Metropolitan Police Force, but its name lived on in the magnificent police station and Magistrates court that now occupy the site.

In place of filth, starvation, and degradation, the prisons were models of a new kind of equally oppressive regime. In the "silent system," prisoners spent most of their time alone in their cells, stripped of their personal identity, known only by a number, and dressed in prison uniform.

Right: Local police stations were usually live-in affairs with police staff domiciled on site. They were an important element in the hierarchy of Victorian crime fighters.

system," prisoners spent most of their time alone in their cells, stripped of their personal identity, known only by a number, and dressed in prison uniform. Their punishment was manual labour, the "hard" labour of rock breaking and excavation for serious criminals, while shorter-term prisoners and men convicted of less serious offences learned various menial trades, such as shoe mending.

Despite the gradual modernization that was instigated in the penal system, the courts, and the police force in the mid-nineteenth century, famous miscarriages of justice continued to occur. As we know, Conan Doyle himself was instrumental in having Oscar Slater and George Edalji released from prison, although his other *cause celebre*, Sir Roger David Casement was executed in Pentonville Prison in 1916.

By the mid-nineteenth century, the Metropolitan Police Force had begun to use various kinds of equipment that would become universally recognizable. The first horse drawn van specifically for transporting prisoners was introduced in 1858. Dark in color, these became known as "Black Marias."

Left: A lithograph of a Black Mariah from the *Illustrated Police News*.

Below: The celebrated Black Mariah discharges its prisoners. The V.R. stands for Victoria Regina, Queen Victoria.

Right: The lurid front page of the *Police News* demands "Two more Whitechapel horrors, when will the murderer be captured?" Note the bull's-eye lamp that the policeman is shining on the victim's face—it is the same type as that illustrated on page 109.

Below: A fragment of one of a number of letters sent to the police, and other authority figures, that claimed to be from Jack the Ripper. As a postscript, the sender adds a final taunt "Catch me if you can." Some of these letters were judged to be authentic, because they contained details of the murders known only to the police and the perpetrator himself.

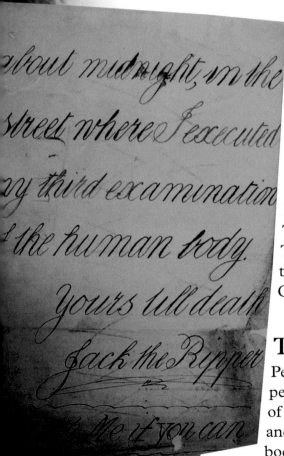

Police officers themselves were also drawn from a higher caliber of recruits as respect for the institution grew. They also became taller, as the standard height for officers was increased to 5 feet 8 inches in 1870 (except in the Thames Division, for some obscure reason). Men at the top of the profession, such as Commissioner Richard Mayne (appointed in 1855), were highly paid; he drew an annual salary of £1,883, a very considerable sum at this time. His two assistant commissioners were paid £800 each. At the same time, Superintendents received £200 per annum; Inspectors were paid £100, Sergeants £58, and Constables a mere 19 shillings each week. The entire organization of the "Met" cost £240,000 a year.

Challenges to the police force were also growing. This was a period of severe unrest and rioting, and 3,200 officers were needed in 1865 to control a serious riot in Hyde Park, central London. Twenty-eight officers were permanently disabled in the fray, and a stone struck even Commissioner Mayne. In the end, the army was called in to restore order. Rather less seriously, there was an epidemic of linen theft from washing lines, and Constables were asked to "call at the houses of all persons on their beats having wet linen in their gardens, and caution them of the risk they run in having them stolen."

1872 saw the first strike by Metropolitan officers, and several men were disciplined (although they were allowed to return to the force). New police stations were continually opened during this period, including New Scotland Yard itself in 1875. Three years later, the Criminal Investigations Department (CID) was established under Charles Vincent, the newly appointed Director of Criminal Investigations.

Further "Divisions" were created in 1879, so that there were a total of 26.

The 1880s were a particularly difficult decade for the Metropolitan police force. As well as encountering extremely serious riots and civil unrest, Scotland Yard itself was bombed by the Fenians in 1884, in an attack targeted on the Special Irish Branch of the force. In 1885, more bombs exploded at both the Tower of London and the Houses of Parliament, and the Trafalgar Square riots of 1886 and 1887 led to the resignation of two police Commissioners (Sir Edmund Henderson and Sir Charles Warren).

True Crime

Perhaps the most serious crisis to face Scotland Yard during this period was case of Jack the Ripper. Between 1888 and 1891, a total of eleven women, mostly prostitutes, were butchered in frenzied and psychotic attacks in the East End district of London. Their bodies were grotesquely mutilated and body parts and organs

POLICE NEWS

THE ILLUSTRATED

LAW COURTS AND WEEKLY RECORD

THE BERNER ST VICTIM.

FIFTH VICTIM

INSPECTOR REID

INQUEST ON FIFTH VICTIM AT ST GEORGES IN THE EAST

TWO MORE WHITECHAPEL HORRORS. WHEN WILL THE MURDERER BE CAPTURED?

BACK OF BERNER STREET

POLICE CONSTABLE WATKINS SIGNALLING FOR ASSISTANCE

MITRE SQUARE ALDGATE   THE FATAL SPOT

THE SCENE ON SUNDAY IN BERNER STREET

FINDING THE BODY IN MITRE SQUARE

THE FIFTH VICTIM OF THE WHITECHAPEL FIEND.

FINDING THE MUTILATED BODY IN MITRE SQARE.

POLICE NOTICE.

TO THE OCCUPIER.

On the mornings of Friday, 31st August, Saturday 8th, and Sunday, 30th September, 1888, Women were murdered in or near Whitechapel, supposed by some one residing in the immediate neighbourhood. Should you know of any person to whom suspicion is attached, you are earnestly requested to communicate at once with the nearest Police Station.

Metropolitan Police Office,
30th September, 1888.

Printed by M'Corquodale & Co. Limited, "Th

Left: The police were so desperate to catch the Ripper, that they issued these posters soliciting help from the public. At this time London's East End was full of people on the wrong side of the law, so the police were doubtful that they would receive much co-operation.

Left: A surgical post-mortem knife of the type thought to have been used by the Ripper. The proximity of the crimes to the London Hospital, and the murderer's skill in dissecting the corpses, suggested a surgical training. This brought various medical men under suspicion.

Right: A cartoon at the time showed a blindfolded policeman, while various hideous effigies (signifying Jack the Ripper), dance around him. This was a popular view and one Holmes may have shared.

> "When I have done another one you can try and catch me again.
> So goodbye dear Boss, till I return.
> Yours, Jack the Ripper."

removed. The Ripper case was the first serial killing ever investigated by the Met, and they had only limited success. Despite a team of officers of the highest rank and calibre being brought in from Scotland Yard to supervise the local division, and a raft of suspects being arrested, no conviction was secured for the murders. Despite over a century of investigation, they remain unsolved to this day. Even worse, "saucy Jack" taunted the police with their failure, submitting jaunty accounts of his "Whitechapel Murders" to the newspapers. The ultimate insult to the police came in October 1888, when the headless torso of one of the victims was discovered in the foundations of the new Whitechapel police headquarters, then under construction.

But although the Ripper murders were the undoubtedly the most notorious crime of this period, the era was marked by a wave of the most violent killings. The poor condition of the economic underclass undoubtedly contributed to the circumstances of many infamous murders. In 1873, an unemployed man named Parker cut the throats of his disabled son and daughter, rather than see them go to the dreaded workhouse. Infanticide amongst London's poorest residents was shockingly commonplace, and it was estimated that one in every 15,000 babies born was murdered soon afterwards. Terrible living conditions were also a factor in several killings. Living with his wife and seven children in a one-room coal cellar, led one Greenwich resident to become so unhinged that he murdered his wife by throwing a knife at her. Depraved by hunger, and "Almost before the breath was out of his mother… (the couple's twelve year old son) was searching about the bed to see if he could find any ha'pence." Then as now, women and children were often the victims of domestic violence, and in the absence of divorce, "deplorable wife

Below: The *Police News* coverage of the 1888 murder of Annie Chapman. The newspaper claims that she was the Ripper's fourth victim, but most authorities maintain that she was actually the second. A number of other murders that occurred before and after the five "core" killings were also attributed to the Ripper.

Left: The front of 29 Hanbury Street, where Annie Chapman was murdered in 1888. Little had changed by the 1950s, when this photograph was taken. At the time of the murder, a Mr. Richardson, a packing crate maker, occupied the shop.

Greenwood takes a more serious view of London's criminality, and ascribes it to "seven curses": neglected children, professional thieves, professional beggars, fallen women, drunkenness, gamblers, and the waste of charity.

JAMES GREENWOOD IN *THE SEVEN CURSES OF LONDON* (1869)

Left: The backyard of Number 29 where this dismembered body was found. Drunks and prostitutes frequented the yard, so suspicious comings and goings went unnoticed. The yard is clearly identifiable in this photograph from the *Police News* (opposite).

Right: Overcrowding, the lack of adequate streetlight, and the "street life" to which many women and children were abandoned, ensured that the poorer parts of nineteenth-century London became hotbeds of vice and crime. Outrages like the Ripper killings were all too easy to perpetrate, and he successfully evaded capture.

Right: A contemporary print of the Ripper murders shows a pair of gentlemen, remarkably like Holmes and Watson, in pursuit of a Ripper suspect. If only Holmes could have turned his attention to this real life horror.

murder" was particularly common. Prostitutes were particularly vulnerable, as were the elderly. Several widows and widowers were murdered in the 1880s, mostly during bungled burglaries.

Murder was by no means the only crime in the wave of offences the police had to deal with. Two contemporary social commentators, Charles Dickens Jr. in his 1879 title, Dickens's *Dictionary of London* and James Greenwood in *The Seven Curses of London* (1869) cover a good array of mid- to late-nineteenth century crime. Dickens concentrates on the so-called "nuisances… to which metropolitan flesh is heir." These included a large variety of offences, including animal baiting, the careless driving of cattle, cock-fighting, furious driving, indecent exposure, obscene singing, and mat beating after 8 a.m.. By contrast, Greenwood takes a more serious view of London's criminality, and ascribes it to "seven curses:" neglected children, professional thieves, professional beggars, fallen women, drunkenness, gamblers, and the waste of charity. As well as the

Above: A selection of poison bottles from the Police Museum collection. Poisoning was a popular means of dispatch in Victorian times, partly because many deadly poisons were easy to obtain and there were few forensic tests to establish their presence in victims' bodies. This gradually changed as the century progressed.

Left: Every home had a cutthroat razor, and they became popular weapons in more "spontaneous" murders.

Below: One of a collection of bizarre knives, used as murder or assault weapons, on show at the Police Museum. Sailors arriving at the London docks would often bring knives like these from overseas, and carry them for self-defense.

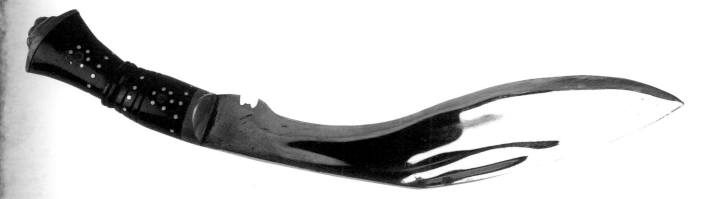

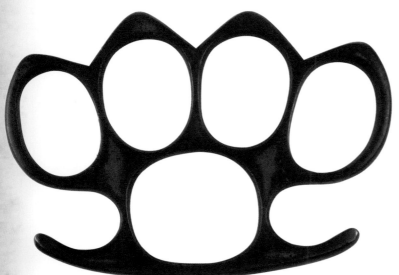

Left: A pair of Victorian brass knuckles. These could be carried in a pocket, and gave the bearer an instant advantage in a street brawl.

Below: A murder weapon concealed in a hollowed-out book, from the Police Museum collection. In "The Solitary Cyclist," the Reverend Williamson hides his revolver in a hollowed out prayer book—see page 178.

Top: A Kukri, originally from India, was one of a number of lethal weapons carried by criminals. The razor sharp blade and curved cutting edge could sever a person's head with a single blow.

Right: Two knives in The Sherlock Holmes Museum collection. The small ivory handled knife is of the type used to murder Mr. Willoughby Smith in "The Golden Pince-Nez." The horn-handled clasp knife is like that used to assassinate Pietro Venucci in "The Six Napoleons."

diverse vices discussed by Dickens and Greenwood, blackmail, terrorism, and attempted suicide were all the province of the over-stretched constabulary.

Sherlock Holmes's cases also reflect the crime-ridden nature of the times, and the fascination that the general public had with criminal activity and detection. Although Holmesian crimes are almost always committed in more ingenious and subtle ways than the common or garden variety, they are often fall into the categories of those committed by more ordinary criminals: murder, attempted murder, bank robbery, burglary, kidnap, treason, and espionage.

In an attempt to stem the tidal wave

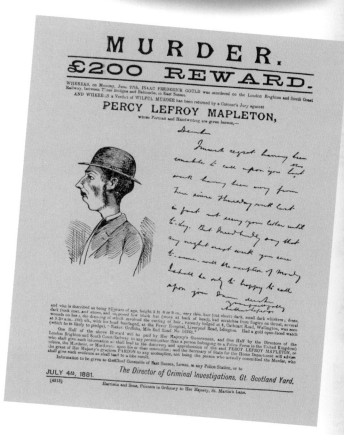

Above: A typical Victorian murder poster offering the princely sum of £200. This would have been equivalent to several years' comfortable income.

Right: Night duty at Marlborough Street Police Station. Reports of robbery, and the arrest of drunks and prostitutes, made this a busy time of day.

Right: By the end of the nineteenth century, police recruitment standards were much more stringent. This resulted in a high caliber of policeman, as demonstrated in this photograph of a fine body of police officers, taken at the Canterbury police station in Kent, England.

Left: Despite the pressures of policing a busy and crowded city like London, Victorian beat officers were not issued with firearms. This tradition persists to this day, despite the high level of gun crime in the city.

The Police, Canterbury Police Station Pound Lane

of real life criminality that hit London in the 1880s and 1890s, an increased number of police officers were recruited to the force. By the end of the century, there were 16,000 serving men in the metropolis, whose job was to police a population of over 7 million Londoners.

Selection procedures to join the force also became more demanding in an attempt to recruit men of a higher caliber. In 1894, potential policemen had to fulfil the following criteria before they could join the force: they had to be over 21 and under 27 years of age, at least 5 feet 9 inches tall in their stockings, able to read and spell, generally intelligent, and free from any bodily complaint. Physical "defects" that might lead to the rejection of a candidate included flat feet, joint stiffness, a narrow chest, or a facial deformity. But despite the improved standard of police recruits, there was unrest in the ranks, as officers began to demand better working conditions. The suicide rate among police officers was particularly high, and this was ascribed to the harsh discipline to which they were subjected. Dismissal and pay docking were commonplace for even minor offences, and the practice of working thirteen days in fourteen meant that officers became exhausted. Gradually, they were granted many of the benefits they requested, including ten days annual holiday, and a boot allowance.

Violence against police officers was also on the increase. Several officers, including Police Constable Baldwin, were murdered in the 1890s. Despite this, calls for the Metropolitan Police to be armed with revolvers were rejected, and "Met" beat officers remain unarmed to this day.

Left: The reassuring police lamp was a common sight in every city district, town, and village in Victorian England.

CHAPTER SIX

"I have never loved, Watson, but if I did and if the woman I loved had met such an end, I might act even as our lawless lion-hunter has done."
SHERLOCK HOLMES, "THE DEVIL'S FOOT"

"I am not a whole-souled admirer of womankind."
SHERLOCK HOLMES, "THE VALLEY OF FEAR"

"Should I ever marry, Watson, I should hope to inspire my wife with some feeling which would prevent her from being walked off by a housekeeper when my corpse was lying within a few yards of her."
SHERLOCK HOLMES, "THE VALLEY OF FEAR"

"The good Watson had at that time deserted me for a wife, the only selfish action which I can recall in our association. I was alone."
SHERLOCK HOLMES, "THE ADVENTURE OF THE BLANCHED SOLDIER"

Sherlock Holmes's Women

Above: A cameo of Dr Watson as a young man. Watson was to marry three times—in sharp contrast to Holmes, who felt marriage might impair his judgment.

Right: Dorr Steele's haunting illustration of the avenging noblewoman from "The Adventure of Charles Augustus Milverton." Despite witnessing the crime, the chivalrous Holmes and Watson allow the guilty woman to escape.

Although Conan Doyle must have taken a conscious decision that his great creation should remain a single man, it would be quite wrong to assume that Holmes's life is free from feminine influence. It seems likely that the author must have reasoned that, as a bachelor, Holmes would not only have the freedom to operate in his inscrutable, unhindered way, but that he would also be at liberty to develop his own personal habits and eccentricities, untrammeled by the molding nature of domestic life. In *The Sign of The Four*, Sherlock himself explains that, "I should never marry myself, lest I bias my judgment."

In a nod to the "normal," hearth-centered life of the period, Conan Doyle makes Watson the complete obverse of the perennial bachelor, Holmes. Thrice married, Watson admits that, from time to time, his domestic life comes between him and his friend: "I had seen little of Holmes lately. My marriage had drifted us away from each other. My own complete happiness, and the home-centred interests which rise up around the man who first finds himself master of his own establishment, were sufficient to absorb my attention." This sounds very much like Conan

Above: Conan Doyle's own mother was such a strong influence in his life, that it seems significant that Holmes is denied a maternal relationship.

Doyle himself speaking, whose two marriages and five children were the bedrock of his life.

Holmes's closest ever brush with matrimony occurs in "The Adventure of Charles Augustus Milverton," when he becomes engaged to Agatha, Milverton's housemaid. Unsurprisingly, this ill-starred romance is actually a ruse to gain entry to the vicious blackmailer's home, enabling Holmes to recover his client's "imprudent" correspondence with an "impecunious young squire."

The other female relationship that seems remarkably absent from Holmes's life, but was of pivotal importance to his creator, is that with his mother. We learn from Holmes that his grandmother was the sister of the French artist, Vernet, but his mother herself is not mentioned in the Canon, and we never learn her name. This fits into a pattern observed by Watson; "I never heard him refer to his relations, and hardly ever to his early life." Holmes's gifted brother Mycroft is the only other member of his family to make an appearance, and they are hardly affectionate with one another. Mention of Holmes's parents is so completely missing from the stories, that it seems safe to assume he is an orphan by the time we meet him. This is in stark contrast to Conan Doyle, whose exceptionally close relationship with his intelligent, artistic mother, "the Ma'am," shaped his life, both personally and professionally. He began a lively correspondence with her when he was away at boarding school in England, and kept up the habit for all of her life. Although Arthur was in his early sixties when she finally died, he was devastated by her loss. Even then, he refused to relinquish their relationship, and kept up "contact" with her in the Spirit World.

Perhaps Conan Doyle deliberately eradicated Holmes's mother to explain his lack of desire for female companionship. He himself was never without a female partner throughout his adult life.

But despite Holmes's ambiguous attitude to women, there are many interesting female characters in the Canon. His female clients, in particular, seem to fascinate the great detective… at least for the duration of their "problem." Watson takes this interest rather further, by marrying Holmes's client Mary Morstam, who brings her dilemma to the attention of the great detective in *The Sign of The Four.*

Regardless of this, Holmes is often condemned as a misogynist, and many of his remarks do seem to support this criticism. Throwaway comments reveal his belief that women are fickle, trivial, unreasonable, and superficial: "Women are never to be entirely trusted – not the best of them;" "When a woman thinks that her house is on fire, her instinct is at once to rush to the thing which she values most… A married woman grabs at her baby – an unmarried one reaches for her jewel box."

But these axioms do not reflect the serious consideration Holmes

"MISS CUSHING."

Above: Holmes displays a "remarkable gentleness and courtesy in his dealings with women."

Right: In "A Scandal in Bohemia," Irene Adler disguises herself as a man to wish Sherlock Holmes "Goodnight." She is the only woman in the Canon that seems to be of sexual interest to Holmes.

gives to the women with whom he becomes involved in his professional work. That he can also read their characters very accurately enables him to solve several cases. Indeed, although Holmes may consider women inferior to men, his empathy with them is surprisingly strong.

Regardless of Holmes's reservations about women, Watson records that he has a "peculiarly ingratiating way with [them]." Although it seems as though Holmes is not attracted to women, he himself seems to exude a magnetic sexual charisma. Certainly, his behavior is almost always chivalrous, and both Watson and Mrs. Hudson remark on his "remarkable gentleness and courtesy in his dealings with women."

Right: One of several photographs thought to be likenesses of Irene Adler.

It would also be quite wrong to assume that Holmes is unappreciative of womanly charm and beauty. He describes the famous Irene Adler as "the daintiest thing under a bonnet on this planet," and quite often refers to the appearance of women he meets in his work. He clearly warms to most of his female clients, such as Lady Eva Bracknell ("the most beautiful debutante of last season"), and the independent Violet Hunter in "The Adventure of the Copper Beeches."

Despite this, Adler is the only woman described in Holmes's casebook who inspires anything like a romantic interest in the detective. Although Watson is keen to refute any romantic relationship, "It was not that he felt any emotion akin to love for Irene Adler," Holmes certainly admires both her beauty and intelligence; "In his eyes she eclipses and predominates the whole of her sex." Subsequent to their meeting in "A Scandal in Bohemia," Holmes freely acknowledges that she is the only member of the fair sex ever to have outwitted him (though Adler herself defers to Holmes as "so formidable an antagonist."). Recalling her simply as "The Woman," Holmes continues to refer to her ability in the course of several other cases.

Below: Holmes admired the independent Violet Hunter in "The Adventure of the Copper Beeches."

In general, Holmes shows his strongest interest in women when they come to him as clients. The more fascinating the dilemma they bring him, the more they seem to arouse his interest. But once their mystery is resolved, they suffer the same fate as his client Violet Hunter. Watson remarks "my friend Holmes, rather to my disappointment, manifested no further interest in her when she had ceased to be the center of one of his problems."

Holmes closest day-to-day relationship with a woman is undoubtedly that which he has with his landlady, the redoubtable Mrs. Hudson. Though, unsurprisingly, she finds him a rather troublesome lodger. His famous disregard for keeping regular hours, his rejection of her cooked meals, his legendary untidiness, the smells caused by his chemical experiments, and the

"I AM SO DELIGHTED THAT YOU HAVE COME."

Above: Of Mrs. St. Clair, Holmes remarks, "I have seen to much not to know that the impression of a woman may be more valuable than the conclusion of an analytical reasoner."

Right: Holmes welcomes Miss Mary Sutherland with the easy courtesy for which he was remarkable.

"atmosphere of violence and danger which hung around him" all combine to make him the "very worst tenant in London." Despite this, Mrs. Hudson demonstrates extraordinary tolerance, and becomes very fond of her wayward lodger. In "The Dying Detective," Watson describes her "genuine... regard" for Holmes, although this is also compounded with a healthy respect for his "masterful" nature. "I didn't dare to disobey him," she says. Although their relationship starts out on a business footing, it certainly becomes far closer over the many years they live together in Baker Street. Indeed, Holmes retains his apartment in her house for over twenty years, even during the post-Reichenbach period of his supposed demise. One could say that she is almost a mother to him.

The fact that Mrs. Hudson had become far more than a landlady to Holmes is particularly evident in "The Empty House," when she risks her life to help him flush out his would-be assassin, and henchman to Professor Moriarty, Colonel Moran. Indeed, her personal devotion to Holmes is such that Mrs. Hudson joins him in his 1903 retirement to practice bee keeping on the windswept Sussex Downs, on England's south coast, far from the smoky comforts of Baker Street.

"Why can't a woman be more like a man?

Why is thinking something women never do?
And why is logic never tried?

PROFESSOR HIGGINS, *My Fair Lady*

Perhaps Holmes basic "problem" with women is, put simply, that they are not like him. He certainly views the female mind as antithetical to his own. Rather than using the "cold clear reason which (he) place(s) above all things," Holmes believes that women rely on their intuition and "emotional qualities." Surprisingly, however, he is not universally critical of this tendency, and understands the value of womanly "instinct." "I have seen too much not to know that the impression of a woman may be more valuable than the conclusion of an analytical reasoner."

Despite his ferocious intellect, Holmes cannot avoid being a man of his times. Men of his generation were conditioned to think of women as weaker and more vulnerable than themselves, creatures who need the protection and guidance of men. Having been brought up to treat women with "gentleness and courtesy," Holmes is particularly appalled by the ill treatment meted out to women at the hands of "bad" men, and is fully aware of the value of a women's honor. Defying the conventions of the day, Holmes also deals directly with his female clients, without seeking a male intermediary or chaperone.

Although a woman governed Britain for most of the nineteenth century, and she was single for most of her adult life, the position of women was still heavily circumscribed in the decades covered by the Canon. As late as 1890, Florence Fenwick Miller, one of the first women to graduate from a British medical school, described the subjugated position of women in shocking terms:

Below: Holmes interviews Miss Mary Holder in "The Beryl Coronet."

"Under exclusively man-made laws women have been reduced to the most abject condition of legal slavery in which it is possible for human beings to be held… under the arbitrary domination of another's will, and dependant for decent treatment exclusively on the goodness of heart of the individual master."

Her description was not far from the truth. Even able and educated women of the privileged classes had no legal identity of their own. On marriage, women were not only obliged to promise to "obey" their husbands, but ownership of their property passed to them. This meant that virtually all wealth was in male hands. Husbands also had extraordinary rights over their wives, even having the legal right to imprison them if they attempted to escape the marital home. Men also had the right to take their children wherever they pleased, even if this was away from their mother.

Inequality was everywhere, even in the divorce laws. A woman could not divorce her husband on the grounds of adultery, but he could divorce her if she was unfaithful to him.

High-status women had almost no career options or opportunities to live independently. Marriage was the only "profession" for which they were educated. Poor women, on the other hand, were often obliged to work, but even their meager wages belonged to their husbands. At this time, nearly all forms of well-paid employment were barred to women, so the lives of most workingwomen consisted of arduous drudgery in domestic service, dangerous factories, or the fields. Many others were forced to prostitute themselves to survive.

Alongside this stark reality of suppression, most men of the higher classes held a strangely idealized view of women. Women were put on a pedestal, almost worshipped, and considered to be made from far "finer clay" than their husbands. Delicate and susceptible as they were, it was considered a man's duty to protect not only his wife, mother and sisters, but all of these feeble creatures. Even women's clothing contributed to this patronizing view of womankind. The huge crinoline-skirted dresses and tight corsets of the late nineteenth century inhibited normal movement and stifled independence.

Holmes certainly displays a protective instinct towards the women who come to him for help, and vigorously shields their interests. But he is also quick to recognize their strengths; Eugenia Ronder's extreme courage in "The Veiled Lodger," and Violet Smith's vibrant energy in "The Solitary Cyclist."

Nearly all the women characters who appear in the Canon are defined by the men in their lives, and many are their victims. But there are exceptions, and several women of an independent stamp are also introduced. Irene Adler made a fortune through her work as a successful opera singer, while Violet Hunter becomes the headmistress of a private school in Walsall, "where I believe that she has met with considerable success." There is also Martha, a "pleasant old lady" in the late-Canon story, *His Last Bow*, who works as his sub-agent in the house of the German spymaster Von Bork.

During the course of Sherlock's career, there was a gradual move to

Above: Holmes is particularly appalled by the bad treatment meted out to woman by depraved men like Enoch J. Drebber of Cleveland, Ohio.

Left: Holmes takes Violet Smith's ungloved hand in "The Solitary Cyclist."

Above: Helen Stoner raises her veil in "The Solitary Cyclist."

emancipate women from many of their shackles. The Married Women's Property Act of 1882 decreed that women could retain rights over their own assets. The Matrimonial Causes Act of 1884 empowered a wife deserted by an adulterous husband to divorce him, and the 1886 reform to the Custody Act meant that a woman was automatically awarded the guardianship of her children if their father died.

Rational and just as he was, it seems highly likely that Holmes would have approved of these sensible measures. Whether he thought that women were cool and rational enough to be awarded the vote (as they were in 1918) is quite another matter...

Left and Right: Eugenia Ronder meets a terrible fate in "The Veiled Lodger" through her husband's jealousy. Victorian women had few rights and were obliged to rely on the chivalry of men. This theme is often reflected in the Holmes stories.

The Traveling Detective

By the time that Sherlock Holmes's career was underway in the 1880s, foreign travel had become an expected part of an upper class Englishman's education.

Although Holmes had not, like Watson, traveled with the army (Watson served in India and Afghanistan), he displays a cosmopolitan awareness of the world throughout his cases. Conan Doyle almost certainly means us to understand that this is an aspect of his personal sophistication. Holmes also demonstrates a willingness to travel, in Britain and abroad, to render his "consulting" services.

In his travels around Britain, Holmes uses

trains quite extensively, and displays an extensive knowledge of railway timetables. George Bradshaw had published his first railway timetable in 1839, and by the 1890s, the familiar yellow wrapper bound "*Bradshaw*" had grown to 946 pages. The late nineteenth century was the era of mass-transit by train, and Holmes made extensive use of them in both Britain and Europe (as shown in Paget's famous illustration of Holmes and Watson in a railway carriage). They also make good use of the ubiquitous Hansom cab in the course of their adventures around London. At the peak of their popularity, over 3,000 Hansoms worked the streets of the capital. Public transport, in the form of horse-drawn omnibuses and the London Underground "tube" train network was also available.

But Holmes's knowledge is not confined to Britain. He also displays a strong interest in, and an extensive knowledge of more far-flung locations, including the American continent. American characters make regular appearances in the Canon, and Holmes assumes the disguise of an Irish-American, Altamont (using his father's middle name), in "His Last Bow." To achieve a convincing persona, we are told that the great detective spent time in Buffalo,

Left: The Victorian era was the first to see widespread travel, due to the great expansion of the railways. Here, Holmes and Watson embark for Switzerland.
Above: Two leather-bound versions of Bradshaw's famous railway timetables. One covers the United Kingdom, and the other is for international travel. Guides like these were vitally useful to Holmes.
Opposite: Sidney Paget's famous illustration of Holmes and Watson in a comfortable railway carriage. It is taken from "The Adventure of Silver Blaze." The duo would often use the time they spent traveling by train to review a case.

Left: City sophisticates Holmes and Watson study the occupant of a Hansom cab.

Above: Hansom cabs were a popular means of public transport, and were often favored by Holmes and Watson.

Above: Holmes adopts the guise of an American, Altamont, in "His Last Bow," using mannerisms acquired on his travels there. He is described as looking like a caricature of Uncle Sam.

Chicago, and Skibbareen, County Cork. Famous Sherlockian, William Baring-Gould, suggested in his erudite biography, *Sherlock Holmes of Baker Street, A Life of the World's First Consulting Detective*, that Holmes's intimate knowledge of America came from time he had spent there as a student, traveling the country with a theater troupe. This would certainly explain his familiarity with stage make-up and the art of disguise.

Conan Doyle himself had first toured America in 1894, working the literary lecture circuit. He was by no means the first British writer to have success there. Charles Dickens had first traveled to the United States in 1842. He not only wrote extensively about this "republic of my imagination" in his book *American Notes*, but also sent one of his characters, Martin Chuzzlewit for an extended visit to the ironically named Eden (actually a disease-ridden settlement where he almost loses his life). This implied criticism did not endear Dickens to his generous hosts. William Thackeray, the famous novelist who had taken the young Conan Doyle onto his knee, had

followed Dickens's example in 1852 lecturing around American on the subject of the English Humorists. Careful not to arouse the hostility of his patrons as Dickens had done, Thackeray repeated this lucrative experience a few years later, delivering his paper on *The Four Georges* (the Hanoverian kings of Britain).

Indeed, the solution of Holmes's first ever "written up" case, *A Study in Scarlet* hinges on events that have taken place on the Mormon Trail to the West, and in Utah itself. The story includes a less than flattering portrait of Brigham Young, "The Moses of America," and one of the founders of the Church of Jesus Christ of the Latter-Day Saints. In using America as a setting

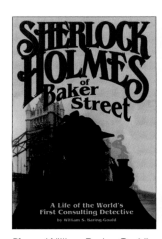

Above: William Baring-Gould's erudite biography, *Sherlock Holmes of Baker Street*.

Above and right: The main action of *A Study in Scarlet* takes place in the "Great Alkali Plain," where John and Lucy Ferrier fall in with the Mormons.

Opposite: Paddington Station, one of London's great railway termini, was quite close to Holmes's and Watson's residence in Baker Street. They would certainly have embarked for many of their out-of-town adventures from here.

for his work, Conan Doyle was very much following the fashion of the period. To his British readers, America was both exotic and yet strangely familiar. English speaking, but not part of the Empire. Although a constant stream of British immigrants arrived in the United States during this period, two-way travel was both time-consuming and expensive and was mostly limited to people of means.

It also seems pertinent that Conan Doyle chooses to explore a particularly uncharted part of the American West in his narrative. The (fictional) Great Alkali Plain is a wild setting for a corrosive mix of religion and violent seduction that plays out in the sad story of John and Lucy Ferrier.

More in the style of the "Grand Tour" of previous centuries, Holmes also travels widely on the Continent. By the 1880s, train travel had made Europe far more accessible, although travel to the Continent was still largely the preserve of the middle and upper classes. During his travels, Holmes visits many of the places popularized by the wealthy gentlemen travelers of the previous century, and the names of familiar European spas and tourist destinations pepper the Canon.

As well as recuperating at Lyons (now Lyon) in France in "The Reigate Squires," Holmes and Watson make a circuitous European tour in "The Final Problem." In an attempt to evade Moriarty and his dangerous followers, they travel through France, Belgium, Germany, and Switzerland. During their tour, the pair visit Dieppe, Brussels, Strasburg, Baden, Geneva, Lausanne, the Rhone Valley, Leuk, the Gemmi Pass, Interlaken, Meiringen (home of the Sherlock Holmes Museum since 1981), and the ill-omened falls at Reichenbach.

In 1893, the Conan Doyles had spent several months at Davos in Switzerland, for the sake of Touie's failing health. Its cool clean air had made the town a Mecca for the rich and ailing. German novelist Thomas Mann was to set his 1924 masterwork, *Der Zauberberg* (The Magic Mountain) in a Davos sanatorium. Like Conan Doyle, Mann also visited the area with his tubercular wife.

During his stay, the athletic Conan Doyle became one of the first English people to learn how to ski downhill, using a pair of skis he had ordered from Norway. Skiing with local residents, the English Branger brothers, he

Right: Conan Doyle, like his creation Sherlock Holmes, was an experienced traveler. The town of Davos in Switzerland erected a plaque to Conan Doyle for greatly enhancing the town's reputation abroad. He wrote a famous article about his sojourn there.

famously traversed the fourteen miles of the Mayerfelder-Furka Pass on May 23, 1894. He became passionate about the activity, and his considered opinion was that "On any man suffering from too much dignity, a course of skis would have a fine moral effect." In 1899, he wrote an article about his skiing experiences in Davos, which greatly stimulated British tourism to the resort. It has remained a popular destination for British skiers ever since. So great was the gratitude of the townspeople of Davos, that they erected a plaque dedicated to Conan Doyle, thanking him for "bringing this new sport and the attraction of the Swiss Alps in winter to the attention of the world."

The Conan Doyle family also stayed in the genteel little town of Meirgingen, probably at the Park Hotel du Sauvage. From here, the family made a trip to visit the local sights, including the Reichenbach Falls. (Holmes and Watson stay at the same hotel in "The Final Problem," although it is renamed the Englisher Hof.) With a drop of 820 feet, the waterfalls at Reichenbach are the most dramatic in the Bernese Oberland, and Conan Doyle fell under the spell of its "dreadful cauldron." The Norwegian Explorers of Minnesota, and the Sherlock Holmes Society of London erected a plaque adjacent to the Falls in 1957, to commemorate the supposed demise of the great detective and the destruction of his great foe Moriarty in "The Final Problem."

Holmes also mentions trips he has taken to some rather more exotic destinations, during his "off-stage" activities, including Ukrainian Odessa, and Trincomalee in Ceylon (modern Sri Lanka). Both of these journeys were undertaken in the course of 1888 cases. At the time, Odessa was the largest port on the Black Sea, and the fourth city of Imperial Russia. This was a period of great tension between Russia and the Western powers, and Holmes's visit fell only seven years after one of the vicious pogroms against the city's Jewish population. When Holmes visited Ceylon, the island was a still a British colony, but the first signs of a Buddhist-inspired independence movement had just begun in the 1880s. Do these significant dates indicate that Holmes was involved in gathering local intelligence for the British Government?

After his supposed demise at Reichenbach, Sherlock tells Watson (during their reunion in "The Empty House") how he reached Florence a week later, and then "travelled for two years in Tibet… and amused myself by… visiting Lhassa and spending some days with the head Llama." He then traveled to Iran ("Persia") and Sudan, disguised as the Norwegian explorer Sigerson, before coming to rest for some months at Montpelier, in the south of France. He also paid a trip to Grenoble, where the sculptor Oscar

Meunier molds his bust in wax, only for it to be shot at by Colonel Moran.

Again, both Lhassa and Khartoum were flashpoints in the international situation in pre-First World War years, and perhaps Holmes's presence there was not accidental. He certainly acknowledges having been in contact with the Foreign Office with information he gleaned on his travels, and he certainly collaborates with the British Government in his later career. In 1898, and after two years' desperate struggle, Lord Kitchener was to depose the Sudanese Khalifa that Holmes had met in Khartoum during his "short but interesting visit."

Above: Holmes visited Ceylon in the days of the British Raj, when the island looked like this.

Left: Holmes sacrifices his fine bust (sculpted by Oscar Meunier during his visit to Grenoble, France) to draw Colonel Moran's fire in "The Empty House."

Above: Conan Doyle and his family visited the Reichenbach Falls several times. The nearby town of Meiringen, where the Conan Doyles stayed, now has its own Sherlock Holmes Museum.

CHAPTER SEVEN

"It is Always 1895..."

"While Sherlock Holmes might not be 'real,' the impact and influence he has nevertheless had on the lives of many are very real, indeed."
STEVEN T. DOYLE, EDITOR OF THE "SHERLOCK HOLMES REVIEW"

"There are no limits to the possibilities of monomania."
DR. JOHN H. WATSON

Below: The Sherlock Holmes Museum at 221b Baker Street is a perennially popular attraction.

Sherlock Holmes Today

O f all the great characters of fiction, Sherlock Holmes has almost certainly inspired the greatest cult following and the most active veneration. Both continue, completely unabated. Not only are there collections, museums, and places of interest for Sherlockians to visit, but a lively thread of Sherlockiana persists in almost every aspect of contemporary culture.

One of the greatest fascinations experienced by Sherlockians seems to be that exerted by the iconic sitting room at 221B Baker Street. This has engendered many recreations, both public and private. Perhaps the first of these was Michael Weight's design for the 1951 Festival of Britain. The Sherlock Holmes Pub in London's Northumberland Street now houses many of the exhibits that were collected together for this famous reconstruction. Other items were donated to the Conan Doyle Collection in Lucens, Switzerland. As of 1994, The Sherlock Holmes Pub also has a stunning portrait of Arthur Conan Doyle, which was unveiled by his daughter, Dame Jean Doyle.

But the most faithful and complete recreation of the iconic rooms is almost certainly that found at Baker Street's Sherlock Holmes Museum. The Museum was opened to the public in 1990, and was the first to be dedicated to a fictional person. Housed in an exact facsimile of the Hudson/Holmes/Watson establishment 221B, its collection is steeped in a wonderfully authentic atmosphere. The sitting room fire crackles in the grate, the flames glint on the copper coal skuttle, the candles flicker, and gutter, and Holmes and Watson's personal effects litter the apartment. The distant rumble of traffic reminds us that Baker Street has always been a busy London thoroughfare, and would have been equally so during Holmes's tenure. Every exhibit displayed in the Museum relates to articles mentioned in the Canon stories, and this dedication to detail contributes to the uncannily "familiar" feeling of the rooms. For a full visual tour of the Sherlock Holmes Museum in London please see pages 79–85.

Below: The Sherlock Holmes Pub at 10 Northumberland Street, London, is just around the corner from Charing Cross Railway Station.

Perhaps the world's second most famous Holmes Museum is that found at Meiringen in Switzerland, where another replica of the Holmes/Watson sitting room has been constructed in the cellar of the town's English Church. Meiringen is the closest town to the infamous Reichenbach Falls, and is the focus for an annual pilgrimage of Holmes's most devoted followers. Members of Sherlock Holmes societies from around the world converge on the town each year on May 4th, to commemorate the epic struggle between Holmes and Moriarty at the nearby Falls.

The University of Minnesota Libraries can claim not one but two versions of the sitting room at 221B. One full-size and a miniature rendering, created by the late Dorothy Row Shaw. In fact, Minnesota lays claim to the world's largest collection of material relating to Sherlock Holmes and his creator, with a fabulous collection of ove 15,000 items. These include original letters written by Conan Doyle, and the original periodicals in which the Holmes stories appeared. There are also subsidiary collections devoted to Americans with strong Holmesian connections, such as actor William Gillette and illustrator Frederic Dorr Steele. Steele illustrated twenty-nine of the thirty-two post-Reichenbach stories, and fixed the image of Holmes for the American public. Such is Minnesota's reputation that has been bequeathed several major collections of Sherlockiana, including that of early Holmes biographer, Vincent Starrett. Curator Timothy J. Johnson has also prepared an on-line addendum to Ronald B. De Waal's

Opposite: The superb recreation of Holmes's and Watson's sitting room at Baker Street's Sherlock Holmes Museum.

magnum opus, The Universal Sherlock Holmes.

Internationally, there are several other museums that celebrate Holmes, including the Sherlock Holmes Museet of Nykobing, Denmark. Invitingly, the museum promises the visitor not only a "comfortable easy chair," but promises that "smoking is allowed, and usually we can also provide you with a cup of coffee or a beer."

Of the legion active Sherlock Holmes societies around the world, reputed to number at least four hundred, the most famous and prestigious is undoubtedly the Baker Street Irregulars of New York City. Taking their name from Holmes's famous troop of street urchins, the society was founded by Christopher Morley in 1934. As well as having an unbelievably illustrious roll call of members (which has included Franklin Delano Roosevelt, Harry S. Truman, and Isaac Asimov), the BSI sponsors many smaller "Scion Societies" across America, including the Ribston-Pippins of Detroit, the Dancing Men of Providence, the Creeping Men of Cleveland, and the Sound of the Baskervilles. The "Sound" publish the *Ineffable Twaddle* newsletter, and *Beaten's (stet.) Christmas Annual.* Membership of the Baker Street Irregulars is by invitation only, and is conferred on those who have contributed to the study of the great man. Membership is by receipt of the "Irregular Shilling" and is considered a great honor among Sherlockians. The society meets each January for an annual dinner and a weekend of Holmesian celebration and study. In 2007, members met to celebrate Holmes's 153rd birthday. The BSI also publish the *Baker Street Journal*, the oldest Holmesian publication in the world, and described by its producers as "An irregular quarterly of Sherlockiana." The *Journal* is actually a highly scholarly magazine that promotes a deep understanding of the Canon, and of Sherlock Holmes himself, who they deem to be still living.

Above: Vincent Starrett, a leading American authority on Sherlock Holmes, is pictured here in 1914, working as a war correspondent in Mexico.

Members of the Sherlock Holmes Society of London also play "The Game" (whereby both Holmes and Watson are considered real people, and still living). It comes from a phrase spoken by Holmes himself, "Come, Watson, come! The game is afoot!" Founded in 1950, the society was a revival of a smaller, pre-war club (founded in 1934), whose distinguished members had included Dorothy L. Sayers. As well of publishing the scholarly *Sherlock Holmes Journal*, the Society has also played an active role in commemorating Holmes around the world, and erecting statues in his honor. The London statue stands, nearly nine feet tall, just outside Baker Street tube station, while the Swiss Holmes sits in pensive bronze in Meiringen's Conan Doyle Place. There are many other British clubs and societies, including the enchantingly named Poor Folk Upon the Moors. This is the Sherlock Holmes Society of the South West of England. Of course, this area is widely featured in the Canon, as

Above: Famous Sherlock Holmes fan Franklin Delano Roosevelt was a member of the Baker Street Irregulars club of New York City.

Above: The recreated drawing room at The Sherlock Holmes Museet located in Nykobing, Denmark.

the setting of Baskerville Hall, "Silver Blaze", and "The Devil's Foot".

Commemorating the fifteen Canon characters that either come from, or have visited Australia, there are several Sherlock Holmes societies there. These include The Sydney Passengers, The Sherlock Holmes Society of Australia, The Sherlock Holmes Society of Melborne (stet.), and the Elementary Victorians. New Zealand has The Antipodean Holmesian Society, based in Denedin.

Europe is also fertile ground for clubs and societies that celebrate the great detective. Olaf H. Maurer founded the 221B: Deutscher-Sherlock-Holmes-Club in 1995, while the Societe Sherlock Holmes de France is very active. The Italian club, Uno Studio in Holmes, honors the great detective's 1891 visit to the country on his escape from Switzerland. Denmark has its Danish Baker Street Irregulars (founded in 1951), whose prospective members must submit a Sherlockian article to the club's newsletter, *Sherlockiana*. Elsewhere in Scandinavia, Sweden has its Baskerville Hall Club, and Norway its Sherlock Holmes Society. Lisbon, Portugal is home to The Norah Creina Castaways, while Barcelona, Spain has its Circulo Holmes. Madrid is home to The Amateur Mendicant

Society of that city. Unsurprisingly, Meiringen in Switzerland has an especially active Holmes Society, the appropriately named Reichenbach Irregulars. In the wider European community, Israel has the Sherlock Holmes Society of Jerusalem, The Ural Holmesian Society is based in the Russian Federation, the Czech Republic has the Ceska spolecnost Sherlocka Holmese, and the delightfully named Seventeen Steppes reside in Kyrgystan.

The Japanese show their fascination with everything English with a cult following of the great detective. There are over twenty-five active Sherlock Holmes societies in Japan. These include the Baritsu Society, the Gacho Club, the Japanese Cabinet, the Men with the Twisted Konjo, and the Tokyo Nonpareil Club. Asia is also home to Malaysia's Common Loafers (founded in 1998), and the Sherlock Holmes Society of India, which is based in New Delhi. The world of cyberspace boasts the Hounds of the Internet.

The web is also home to a fantastic range of Sherlockiana, forming a worldwide community of Holmesians. It is extraordinary that a character suspended in such a specific time and place continues to have such a magnetic appeal to the web generation. It would be impossible to catalog the vast and fluid number of Sherlockian websites, but some of the best are The Baker Street Blog, A Study in Sherlock, HenryZecher.com's Sherlock Holmes, and the Sherlock Holmes Society of London website.

As well as these conventional channels of admiration for Sherlock, there are also some more unusual tribute groups.

The Mini-Tonga Scion Society of New York's Baker Street Irregulars is dedicated to celebrating the "world of Sherlock Holmes in miniature." The Society is named for Tonga, the tiny but deadly native of the Andaman Islands in *The Sign of Four*. Mini-Tonga members create room box versions of famous scenes from the Canon in doll-sized miniature. The sitting room at 221B is the group's most popular subject. Their work is fantastically detailed and authentic, and some of these diminutive room sets have taken decades to complete. As Holmes himself said, "To a great mind, nothing is little."

By contrast, The Irregular Special Players are a group of English actors dedicated to celebrating Holmes's work by performing specially devised cases at Murder Mystery Events. Another "living" memorial to the great man is the Silver Blaze Sweepstakes, an annual horserace run at Denmark's Aalborg Race Track.

Below: *The Sherlock Holmes Journal* is just one of a plethora of periodicals devoted to the great detective.

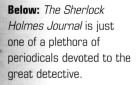

A fantastic range of collectibles and artefacts has also grown up around the Sherlock Holmes legend. For the philatelist, there is now a wide range of postal stamps to collect. This tradition began in 1972, when Nicaragua launched a series of twelve stamps, commemorating the world's most famous detectives to celebrate the fiftieth anniversary of Interpol. Several other countries went on to honor Holmes on their postal stamps, including Britain, Canada, Bhutan, Guernsey, and San Marino. South Africa was the most recent country to do so, in 2000.

Over the years, a great deal of Holmesian memorabilia has been launched, and this has spanned every degree of good and bad taste. As well as the usual gifts and novelties; Holmes teddy bears, Holmes and Watson cruet sets, tea towels, teapots, puzzles, t-shirts, cufflinks, walking sticks, statues, busts, letter openers, fridge magnets, tobacco, pipes, and matches…

Below: The British Royal Mail issued a set of five commemorative Holmes stamps. Each celebrates a different case.

SHERLOCK HOLMES & DR. WATSON "THE REIGATE SQUIRE"   SHERLOCK HOLMES & SIR HENRY "THE HOUND OF THE BASKERVILLES"   SHERLOCK HOLMES & LESTRADE "THE SIX NAPOLEONS"   SHERLOCK HOLMES & MYCROFT "THE GREEK INTERPRETER"   SHERLOCK HOLMES & MORIARTY "THE FINAL PROBLEM"

there are some more unusual novelties including a charming syringe pen, a complete detective kit, and a Professor Moriarty toilet seat. Britain's Traditional Games Company retails a Holmes chess set, which features the great man as the white king, as well as Watson, Moriarty, Mrs. Hudson, Colonel Moran, Irene Adler, and the Hound of the Baskervilles itself (who plays as a knight).

But perhaps the most surprising legacy of Holmes's personality cult is the massive volume of literature that has grown up around him. Legions of books, pamphlets, periodicals, Holmes Society publications, and a huge body of apocryphal fiction have all been published about the great man.

Above: The Traditional Games Company's handsome chess set is based on characters from the Holmes stories.

"There, upon a shelf was the row of formidable scrapbooks and books of reference which many of our fellow-citizens would have been so glad to burn."

DR. WATSON, "THE EMPTY HOUSE"

"Never has so much been written by so many for so few."

CHRISTOPHER MORLEY, SHERLOCKIAN

Below: A set of twenty-seven cigarette cards from the 1930s. Each is based on a different Holmesian character.

A great tradition of scholarship has grown up around Holmes and Conan Doyle's writing, which can trace its heritage back to Vincent Starrett's 1933 title, *The Private Life of Sherlock Holmes*. While Starrett makes gives us a fascinating insight into Holmes's subtle and fascinating world, he is careful to avoid the wild speculations in which other writers have indulged; such as Holmes and Watson have a homosexual relationship, or Holmes is really Jack the Ripper... Famous American Sherlockian, William Baring-Gould continued in Starrett's footsteps with some of the most highly regarded books about Holmes, *The Annotated Sherlock Holmes*, and the excellent fictional biography of the great man, *Sherlock Holmes of Baker Street, A Life of the World's First Consulting Detective*. Rather than making wild speculations about the aspects of Holmes's life that are not revealed by the Canon, Baring-Gould makes educated guesses strongly based on the facts as revealed by Conan Doyle. More recently, Ronald B. De Waal has launched a web version of his massive project, *The Universal Sherlock Holmes* (1994). The book is the third "volume" in a series of bibliographies documenting

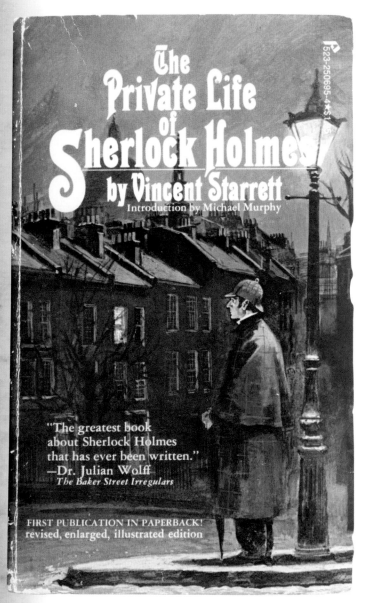

Above: The author's prized copy of Vincent Starrett's 1933 classic, *The Private Life of Sherlock Holmes.*

Above: August Derleth, an admirer of Holmes, created his own detective, Solar Pons, as an homage.

the intricate world of Holmes and Watson.

Less erudite, but equally fascinating is the wealth of Holmes fiction that has kept Conan Doyle's characters alive, even after the author's death. There were two early instigators of post-mortem Holmes pastiches. These were Arthur's son and literary executor Adrian Conan Doyle (1910-1970), and the (extremely prolific) American writer August Derleth (1909-1971). Derleth had corresponded with Conan Doyle, asking if, seeing that Doyle had abandoned the character, he could take over the job as Holmes's "biographer." Conan Doyle politely declined, but Derleth was undeterred, and despite the fact that he had never been to London, he decided to write a series of "homages" to the great detective he so admired. His first Solar Pons title, *In Re: Sherlock Holmes* was published in 1945. However, whereas Solar Pons is obviously based on Sherlock, (he shares his lodgings at 7B Praed Street with his companion Dr. Lyndon Parker and their redoubtable housekeeper Mrs Johnson, and also has an elder, gifted, brother, Bancroft Pons), he is not actually Holmes, who also appears in Derleth's novels. Ironically, like his senior fictional partner, Pons has also inspired fervent admiration, and his own groups of followers. The Praed Street Irregulars was formed in 1966, and a British branch was also spawned, the London Solar Pons Society. *The Solar Pons Gazette* began publication in 2006. When Derleth died, the Solar Pons "franchise" was taken over by Basil Copper. Between them, the two writers produced far more stories about their hero than Conan Doyle ever had about his.

Adrian Conan Doyle's stories, on the other hand, continue with the characters bequeathed to him by his father, including Holmes, Watson, and Lestrade. Not only did he work at the very desk at which his father had sat to write the Sherlock Holmes stories, but his "Aventures" are strongly referenced to cases mentioned in his father's original work. Between 1952 and 1953, Adrian wrote a further twelve Holmesian stories, some with the collaboration of John Dickson Carr (the famous American mystery writer). These were collected and published in 1954, as *The Exploits of Sherlock Holmes.*

PORTRAIT SKETCHES OF SUPPOSED WHITECHAPEL MONSTER AND INCIDENTS IN THE CASE.

Derleth and Doyle were the forerunners of an extensive literary tradition that has grown to include the work of over a hundred writers, and over seven hundred titles, with various degrees of creative success. Several serious and highly respected novelists have taken up the baton, including Isaac Asimov, Colin Dexter, Michael Hardwick, Stephen King, and Dorothy L. Sayers, while many aspiring writers have used Holmes as their inspiration.

If imitation really is the sincerest form of flattery, then Conan Doyle has certainly been heaped with adulation.

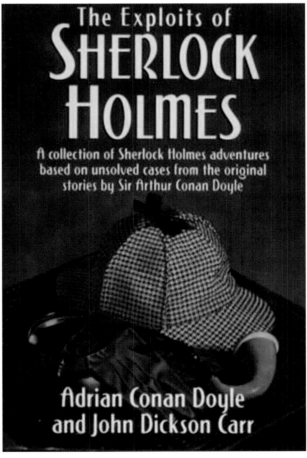

The Exploits of SHERLOCK HOLMES

A collection of Sherlock Holmes adventures based on unsolved cases from the original stories by Sir Arthur Conan Doyle

Adrian Conan Doyle and John Dickson Carr

Above: One of the more bizarre suggestions made by Holmesian scholars is that the great detective was Jack the Ripper. As the sketches on this Police News chart show, the Ripper was thought to be of respectable appearance. Certainly, several professional men became suspects. If not a surgeon or lawyer, why not a consulting detective?

Left: Adrian, Sir Arthur's Conan Doyle's son, wrote a further twelve stories based on the characters and plots bequeathed to him by his father.

Sherlock Holmes's Paraphernalia

Of all the characters in fiction, Sherlock Holmes is perhaps the most closely identified with his personal paraphernalia. Of these, the most famous items are his pipe, costume of deerstalker hat and Inverness cape, magnifying glass, revolver, and his beloved violin, the "Strad."

Strangely, although these accoutrements are now inextricable from our modern image of Holmes, Conan Doyle does not mention any of them (apart from the violin and magnifying glass) in the specific forms in which we now recognize them. Although several of Holmes's key possessions are briefly mentioned in the stories, their significance has been greatly aggrandized with the passage of time.

The Pipe

Holmes's iconic pipe, for example, is simply described by Conan Doyle as an "old and oily clay pipe." But through the many illustrations and interpretations of the Holmes character, the great detective's pipe has gradually transformed into an elaborate, exaggeratedly curved monstrosity. This is not to detract from the importance of smoking to Holmes. In the stories, Watson describes him as being a slave to

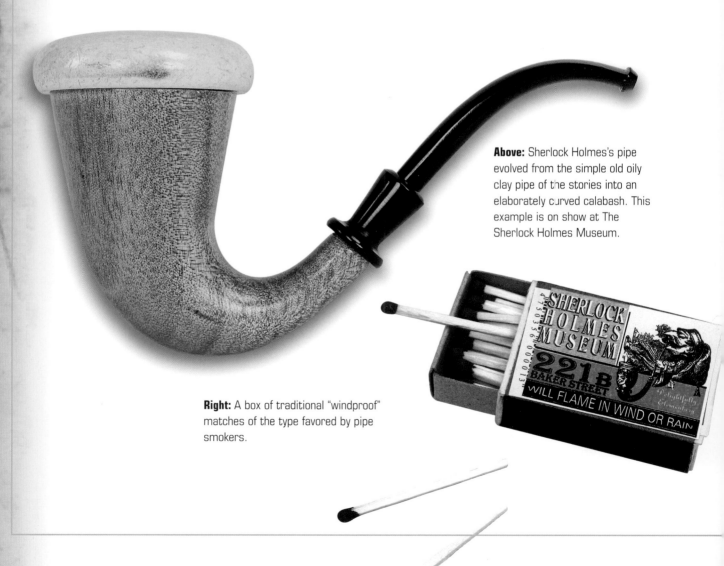

Above: Sherlock Holmes's pipe evolved from the simple old oily clay pipe of the stories into an elaborately curved calabash. This example is on show at The Sherlock Holmes Museum.

Right: A box of traditional "windproof" matches of the type favored by pipe smokers.

Above: A curved briarwood pipe made by Petersons of Dublin. It is likely that, like many pipe smokers, Holmes had several pipes.

problem in pipe-lengths (i.e. the length of time it takes to smoke a pipe), as in "it is quite a three pipe problem." Watson remarks on Holmes often being shrouded in "thick blue cloud-wreathes" and notes with some asperity that the detective is a "self-poisoner by cocaine and tobacco."

It was actually the original Sherlockian actor, the American William Gillette, who introduced a magnificent calabash pipe to the character. A calabash is an ornately carved and deeply curved pipe, whose tobacco bowl is made from

tobacco, which he uses as both a stimulant and an aid to concentration. In fact, Holmes uses tobacco in all its forms, including cigarettes and cigars (for which he keeps a cigar-case). But he obviously favors the reflective quality of pipe smoking. He often measures the obduracy of a

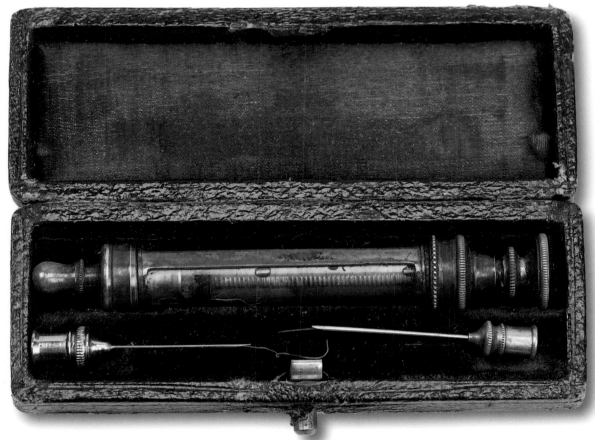

Above: Holmes's hypodermic syringe, used for the self-administration of cocaine and morphine.

Below: Holmes kept his tobacco in a Persian slipper hung on the mantelpiece at 221b.

Bottom: Sherlock Holmes's engraved silver cigarette case.

a hollowed out gourd. Gillette quite deliberately chose this particular style of pipe as a prop for his "Sherlock," as it can be smoked "hands free." Many later Sherlockian actors adopted it for the same reason.

For his own pleasure, Holmes smoked Black Shag, which he acquired by the pound from his tobacconist, Bradley's. Watson's taste was for "Ship's" tobacco, which was blended in the Netherlands, and was the favorite of many sailors. Holmes notes that his friend also smokes an Arcadia blend (which he recognizes by its distinctive ash), and is familiar to him from Watson's bachelor days.

Interestingly, Holmes's passion for tobacco led him to compose a published monograph about the forensic properties of the substance, *Upon the Distinction Between Ashes of the Various Tobaccos.* In this paper, Holmes minutely describes the properties of 140 different

tobacco ashes. Presumably, he was obliged to smoke all 140 varieties, which he probably enjoyed.

Holmes's "Costume"

Although the deerstalker has also become synonymous with the image of Holmes, it was actually Sidney Paget, not Conan Doyle, who introduced both the famous hat and distinctive "Inverness cape" to the character. In fact, in his first ever Sherlock Holmes story, "A Study in Scarlet," Conan Doyle describes the young Holmes as wearing an "ulster," a loose overcoat popular at the time. The deerstalker first appeared in a drawing created by Paget to illustrate "The Boscombe Valley Mystery," and did not appear again for another nine stories, until his classic illustration of Holmes and Watson in a railway carriage for "Silver Blaze."

While Holmes is seen equipped with his iconic "ear-flapped traveling cap," the drawing shows Watson wearing his trademark headwear as well, a rather less flamboyant bowler.

Although Conan Doyle mentioned neither the deerstalker nor the cape, the combination of these two items of apparel would have been quite a la mode for the out-of-town Victorian gentleman. Typically, the versatile deerstalker was worn for country pursuits. It was highly practical; the brims (front and back) provided protection from the sun, the

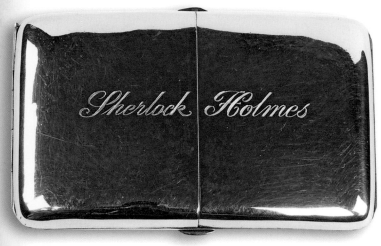

Sherlock Holmes

Left: Holmes's deerstalker first appeared in Paget's illustration for "The Boscombe Valley Mystery."

earflaps kept out the cold, and the checkered twill fabric afforded a measure of camouflage. The Inverness cape was both warm and water resistant, making it ideal for the British climate. It is a sleeveless coat with a cape attached, often fashioned from Harris Tweed and produced in the Scottish Highlands. But a fastidious man like Sherlock Holmes (Watson reflects on his "quiet primness of dress") would never have committed the faux pas of wearing this hearty country garb in town. Paget fully understood this and only ever showed Holmes wearing the cape and hat in rural settings. In *The Hound of the Baskervilles*, for example, Holmes wears a tweed suit and cloth cap, which he certainly would not sport in London. Watson describes Holmes's town attire as consisting of a frock-coat, ulster, and, at home, a dressing-gown (variously described as mouse-colored, blue, or purple), while his usual country wear consisted of a tweed suit worn with a "long gray traveling cloak [and] traveling cap." His town headgear would have been a top hat or bowler.

Although Paget invented Holmes's signature costume, it was William Gillette's interpretation of the role that cemented the Sherlock image in the public imagination (on both sides of the Atlantic). In May 1899, the actor traveled to England, where he was met by Conan Doyle.

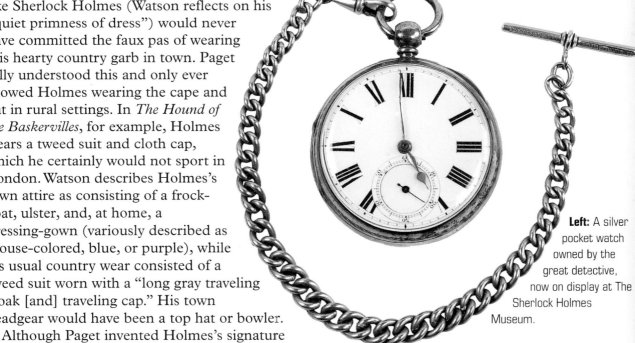

Left: A silver pocket watch owned by the great detective, now on display at The Sherlock Holmes Museum.

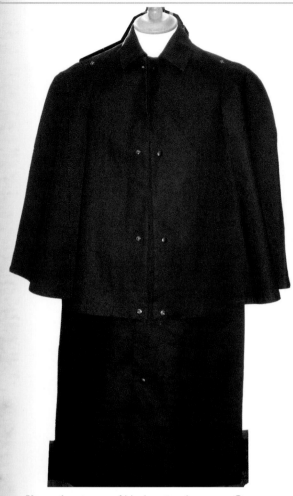

Above: A waterproof black cotton Inverness Cape. Originally worn by Highland regiments, the cape was particularly useful for bandsmen, such as drummers and pipers, as the sleeveless design allowed free movement of their arms, which meant that they could play their instruments even in severe weather. The capes are also manufactured in Harris Tweed for extra warmth.

Above: A framed photograph of Sherlock Holmes from the Museum's collection. Queen Victoria gave Holmes the emerald tiepin on the left in gratitude for "services rendered."

Gillette greeted the author dressed as Holmes complete with hat, cape, pipe, and magnifying glass, with which he proceeded to examine the creator of the great detective. "Unquestionably an author," announced Gillette. Conan Doyle roared with laughter and the pair formed a lifelong friendship.

Ironically, Holmes's supposed "patronage" of the deerstalker and Inverness cape may well have extended the fashionable life of both items. Indeed, they continue to be worn today. The freedom that the sleeveless Inverness gives to the arms has made it particularly popular with bagpipers, and it is now worn over kilts as part of the traditional Highland dress.

Left and above: Two personal items from Dr. Watson's room at 221B, his doctor's bag and bowler hat.

The Magnifying Glass

Another enduring image of Holmes is that of him peering through a magnifying glass. Introduced to the character by Doyle, ("As he spoke, he whipped a tape measure and a large round magnifying glass from his pocket."), the glass was first illustrated by D.H. Friston in the four drawings he produced for the famous *Beeton's Christmas Annual* of 1887. Early Holmesian actor William Gillette, also used it as part of his stage business, and later interpreters of the role continued to use it. This key accoutrement is now ingrained in our collective image of the great detective.

The "Strad"

Violin playing was a popular pursuit in the Victorian era. But Holmes is not a man to take up a pastime lightly and as Watson says, he "plays the violin well." He certainly takes his

Above: Two examples of Victorian magnifying glasses from the desk of the great detective. One has a turned rosewood handle and the other an ivory one.

Left: Holmes's sword cane, a useful weapon on the mean streets of Victorian London.

Above: Holmes's beloved Stradivarius, whose soothing strains concentrated his mental processes.

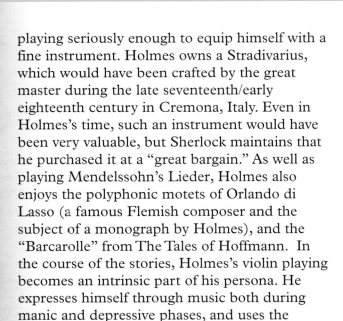

playing seriously enough to equip himself with a fine instrument. Holmes owns a Stradivarius, which would have been crafted by the great master during the late seventeenth/early eighteenth century in Cremona, Italy. Even in Holmes's time, such an instrument would have been very valuable, but Sherlock maintains that he purchased it at a "great bargain." As well as playing Mendelssohn's Lieder, Holmes also enjoys the polyphonic motets of Orlando di Lasso (a famous Flemish composer and the subject of a monograph by Holmes), and the "Barcarolle" from The Tales of Hoffmann. In the course of the stories, Holmes's violin playing becomes an intrinsic part of his persona. He expresses himself through music both during manic and depressive phases, and uses the "Strad's" soothing strains to concentrate his mental powers.

The "Old Favorite" Revolver

Watson mentions that he and Holmes are armed with revolvers or pistols in twenty-one

Canon stories (he uses the terms interchangeably), and the stories themselves refer to guns, pistols, and revolvers over a hundred times. Despite this, the duo are only credited with actually using their weapons on five occasions:

☞ Both Holmes and Watson fire on the Andaman Islander in *The Sign of Four*.

☞ Holmes and Watson both fire at the *Hound of the Baskervilles*.

☞ Watson fires at the mastiff in the "Adventure of the Copper Beeches."

☞ Watson pistol-whips would-be assassin Colonel Moran in the "Adventure of the Empty House."

☞ Holmes pistol-whips Killer Evans in the "Adventure of Three Garridebs," after Watson is shot and wounded.

Above: Holmes's "Old Favorite" revolver is not specifically identified, but most authorities have opted for the Webley Mark III.

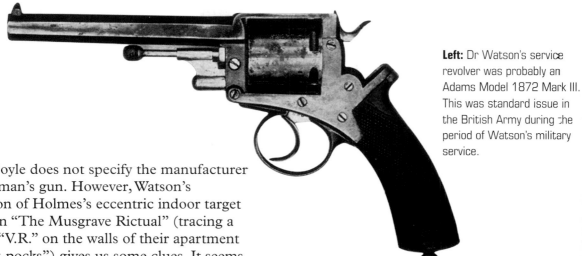

Left: Dr Watson's service revolver was probably an Adams Model 1872 Mark III. This was standard issue in the British Army during the period of Watson's military service.

Conan Doyle does not specify the manufacturer of either man's gun. However, Watson's description of Holmes's eccentric indoor target practice in "The Musgrave Rictual" (tracing a patriotic "V.R." on the walls of their apartment "in bullet-pocks") gives us some clues. It seems likely that Holmes would have used a smaller bore target pistol for such a pursuit, such as the single-shot Webley Model 1880. For more serious case-work Holmes's would have carried his "Old Favorite" revolver. This is described as using "Boxer Cartridges," and having a "Hair-Trigger." At this time, "Boxer" was a generic term given to a particular type of center-fire cartridge; the original having been invented by Colonel Boxer of the British Army around

1866. This vague description of his weapon is quite pertinent; Holmes is much more interested in the forensic study of ballistics, rather than in firearms themselves. As a well-known patriot, it is very likely that Holmes would have used an English-made revolver (rather than a European model), so a Webley Mark III might be a likely candidate for his firearm.

Left: A civilian Beaumont Adams revolver, also owned by Dr Watson, is displayed in a case at the Sherlock Holmes Museum.

Watson's weapon is described rather more specifically as being an "old service revolver." He would have received it during his years in Afghanistan. In his time of service, it was customary to keep an army-issued weapon on discharge from active duty. We can deduce from Watson's years of enlistment (1879 to 1880), that his gun was most probably the Adams 1872 Mark III center-fire revolver. The Adams was standard issue equipment in the British army between 1878 and 1880, and was never sold

commercially. Based on the earlier Beaumont-Adams percussion revolver (which was widely used during the Civil War), the later gun was both breech loading and double action, using center-fire ammunition that had now become

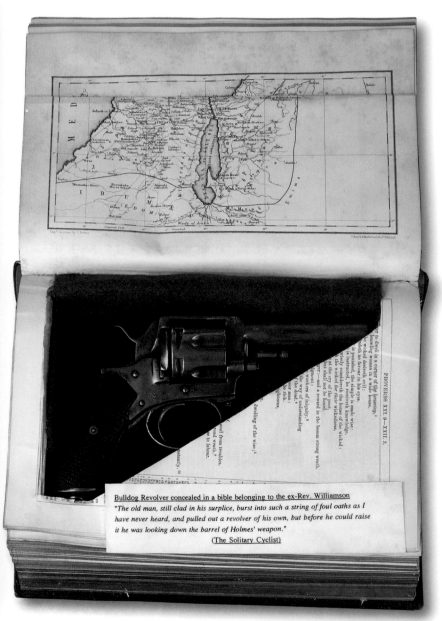

Bulldog Revolver concealed in a bible belonging to the ex-Rev. Williamson
"The old man, still clad in his surplice, burst into such a string of foul oaths as I have never heard, and pulled out a revolver of his own, but before he could raise it he was looking down the barrel of Holmes' weapon."
(The Solitary Cyclist)

Left: A Bulldog revolver concealed in a prayer book, as used by Rev. Williamson in "The Solitary Cyclist."

Above: The Legion D'Honneur awarded to Holmes for services rendered to the French Government.

more widely available. As a .45 caliber, it had excellent stopping power, and six-shot capability.

Watson also describes how he later acquires a Webley revolver, possibly a Mark II Civilian Pocket Model, and this may well hint to Holmes's gun being from the same armory.

Above: Holmes reads a book about bee keeping in preparation for his retirement on the South Downs in the County of Sussex.

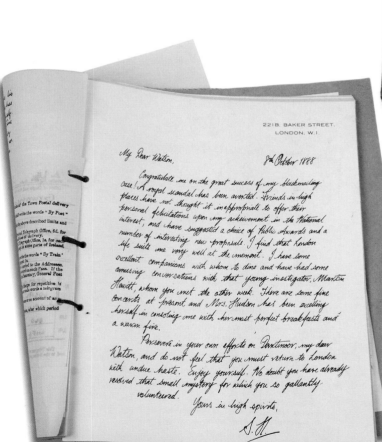

Left: A letter dated October 8, 1888. Holmes writes to Watson from Baker Street. Watson is on Dartmoor, making preliminary enquiries in the case of *The Hound of the Baskervilles*.

Sherlock Holmes Pub

Situated at number 10–11 Northumberland Street, Westminster, London, and known in Holmes's times as The Northumberland Arms, this is where Holmes tracked down Francis Hay Moulton in "The Noble Batchelor."

Old Scotland Yard is just across the other side of Northumberland Avenue, and the Turkish Baths that Holmes and Watson frequented were beside the hotel in Craven Passage. The disused entrance forms part of the wall of the bank. With Charing Cross Station just around the corner, it is not hard to imagine Holmes and Watson hurrying through the foggy streets of London to catch a train to the location of another baffling case. To this day, the pub is filled with artifacts relating to Holmes and his cases. These include the Hound of the Baskerville's stuffed head and there is also a replica of the Holmes/Watson sitting room and study. Diners in the restaurant are able to view this through a large glass partition.

Left: The Inn sign has two aspects, one shows Holmes reading a note, clad in his dressing gown; the other shows him in his deerstalker, examining a clue with his magnifying glass. In both versions, he is smoking furiously.

Left and right: In the bottom panes of the front windows, the likenesses of Holmesian characters are etched into the glass. Originally, there were six, but only four survive. Shown here are the depictions of Sherlock Holmes and Dr. Watson.

Below: The exterior of the pub on a warm summer's day. One wonders whether Holmes and Watson would have approved of *al fresco* dining in shirtsleeves.

CHAPTER EIGHT

Sherlock Holmes on Stage, Screen, and Radio

· · · · · · · · · · · · · · · · · · · ·

Above: An extract from Paget's famous illustration of *The Hound of the Baskervilles*. The book has been filmed more times than any other work of fiction.

Right: American actor William Gillette. For many, he *was* Sherlock Holmes. He also formed a deep rapport with Conan Doyle.

One of the most brilliant aspects of Conan Doyle's writing style is his ability to conjure crystal clear images of his characters and plot action. It is truly "cinematic." Extraordinarily, partly through Conan Doyle's brilliant writing, and partly through Sidney's Paget's glamorous evocation of the great detective, Sherlock became a star before the movies were even invented. He has now become the most-often portrayed fictional character; more than seventy-five actors have taken the role of Holmes in at least 211 movies, since the first Sherlock Holmes peep machine show back in 1911. Holmes's popularity has also resulted in *The Hound of the Baskervilles* being filmed more often than any other work of fiction.

During his lifetime, Conan Doyle himself was fully aware of the stage potential of his character, and brought him to the London stage on several occasions, particularly when his funds were low. But the actor to receive his strongest personal endorsement in the role was the American, William Gillette. Gillette was quite an extraordinary character himself: brought up as a Yankee aristocrat in Nook Farm, Connecticut, he was the childhood friend of Mark Twain. In later life, he built the extraordinary 24-room Gillette Castle, which was featured in *National Geographic's Guide to America's Great Houses*. Although Gillette was often described as a taciturn and difficult character off-stage, he was nevertheless the friend to many powerful and creative people, and struck up a deep rapport with Conan Doyle himself.

Other actors of the period may claim to be the first to portray

Above: Gillette built Gillette Castle, a twenty-four-room mansion in East Haddam, Connecticut. He funded the house with income derived from playing Holmes.

Below: Illustrator Frederic Dorr Steele used Gillette as his model for Holmes.

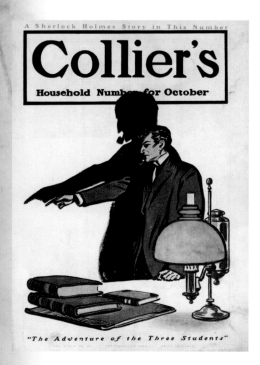

Holmes; the English actor Charles Brookfield co-wrote and performed *Under the Clock* at the London's Royal Court Theatre in 1893, but Gillette *became* the role, and was certainly Conan Doyle's choice for his brilliant detective. Conan Doyle wrote Gillette's original play, *Sherlock Holmes – A Drama in Four Acts*, but Gillette is known to have adapted it extensively until it became his own. The play first opened in New York City in 1899, to rave reviews. Gillette brought it to England in 1901. He was to give over 1,300 stage performances of the role between 1899 and 1932, and revived it for radio in 1935.

Interestingly, on Gillette's 1903 tour of England, the young Charlie Chaplin took the role of Billy.

For many people, William Gillette *was* Holmes, fiction made flesh. He single-handedly created the public image of the great detective, with his calabash, deerstalker, cape, and magnifying glass, and is even credited with coining the seminal phrase, "Elementary, my dear Watson," which never actually appears in the Canon. Gillette was also Frederic Dorr Steele's model for his illustrations of the great detective. For many people who saw Gillette on stage, he appeared to be the embodiment of Holmes in appearance, mannerism, and intensity, the only possible actor in the role. Helen Hayes was one of many famous contemporaries who declared "William Gillette is the only real Sherlock Holmes for me." Eminent Sherlockian Vincent Starrett confirmed that he appeared to be "the living embodiment of Sherlock Holmes." But most astonishingly, Arthur Conan Doyle himself told Gillette "you make the hero of anemic printed page a very limp object as compared with the glamour of your own personality which you infuse into his stage presentment."

Gillette certainly became permanently identified with the character of Holmes, but unlike several later incumbents, he did not object to this. Indeed, it was the cornerstone of his professional reputation and his huge popularity. Ironically, Gillette also wrote a Sherlockian drama of his own, a strange one-act parody entitled *The Painful Predicament of Sherlock Holmes*, in which the great detective does not speak. Despite Holmes's silence, the

play was well received.

Predictably, Gillette's one and only movie was the silent *Sherlock Holmes*, filmed in 1916, although, surprisingly, he was not the first actor to bring Sherlock to the screen. An unknown actor had appeared in a silent picture of 1903, *Sherlock Holmes Baffled*, and Maurice Costello had appeared in 1905's *Adventures of Sherlock Holmes*. But Gillette was the first actor to portray Sherlock on the radio, in 1930. In those early, golden, years of radio, when it was the most widely accessible medium, several other famous actors also took up the role, including Basil Rathbone, Orson Welles, Sir Cedric Hardwicke, Arthur Wontner, and Sir John Gielgud.

On screen, the role changed hands several times in the early years of the twentieth century. Several of these actors are relatively unknown today (including Harry Benham and James Bragington), but working in the early 1920s, Eille Norwood became the first actor since Gillette to be considered a "definitive" Holmes. Between 1921 and 1923 he starred as the great detective in forty-seven silent movies, each of which lasted an average of twenty minutes. They were closely based on Conan Doyle's original stories, and the great author himself praised Norwood's interpretation of the role, "His wonderful impersonation of Holmes has amazed me."

John Barrymore also appeared as Holmes in 1922, in a film version of Gillette's play. On stage, Dennis Neilsen-

Above: Actor Ellie Norwood played Holmes on screen between 1921 and 1923, starring in 47 silent movies.

Below: A movie poster for John Barrymore's 1922 version of Gillette's play.

Above: John Barrymore in a still from the silent movie version of Gillette's play.

Terry portrayed the great detective in Conan Doyle's one-act play *The Crown Diamond*. But the work was not a roaring success; it ran for only three months and was never revived. Conan Doyle cannibalized elements of its plot in the "Adventure of the Mazarin Stone."

When the talkies arrived in the 1930s, a new generation of actors hit the big screen. Arthur Wontner became the first talking Holmes, and in 1931, Robert Rendell played the great detective in the first talking version of *The Hound of the Baskervilles*. Raymond Massey also took the part in this era.

In the 1940s, however, the character of Sherlock was completely dominated by one actor: Basil Rathbone (1892 to 1967). Rathbone had been a war hero in the First World War, and was awarded the British Military Cross. He moved to Hollywood to further his acting career, and was cast as Holmes in 1939. He made fifteen Holmes movies over the next seven years, with Nigel Bruce cast as his Watson, and

Above: A monochrome movie poster for *The Hound of The Baskervilles*. A real Conan Doyle story.

broadcast 242 Holmes radio dramas. But, like Conan Doyle, Rathbone became gradually bored with the character and felt typecast as Holmes. He even conceived a strong personal dislike for the great detective, asserting that "there was nothing lovable about Holmes… his perpetual seeming assumption of infallibility; his interminable success; (could he not fail just once and prove himself a human being like the rest of us!)." Rathbone quit the role in 1946, and returned to the stage work he loved. However, like Conan Doyle, he missed the financial rewards that Holmes had brought him, and decided to make one final reappeared in the character. Rathbone revived Holmes in a play written by his wife, Ouida, but the production was a complete flop and ran for only three performances.

So great was Rathbone's imprint on the role of Holmes that no other movie studio or movie actor would touch it for years, until Peter Cushing was cast in the 1959 remake of *The Hound of the Baskervilles*. The film was produced by English movie studio Hammer Films. Cushing (1913 to 1994) was English, but had arrived in Hollywood in 1939, and landed parts in several films. These included *A Chump At Oxford* in which he starred with Stan Laurel and Oliver Hardy. Cushing served in Britain's Entertainment National Services Association during the war, and then decided to pursue a film career in Britain. Although Cushing also became famous for appearing in various Hammer horror movies, he reappeared as Holmes in 1984 (at the age of 74), in *Sherlock Holmes and the Masks of Death*.

If every decade has its iconic "Holmes," then Christopher Lee is the Holmes of the 1960s. Having appeared as Henry Baskerville in Hammer's *Hound of the Baskervilles*, Lee was cast as Holmes himself in the first color

Above: A still featuring Rathbone and Bruce. Their attire is fairly consistent with the Paget illustrations.

Opposite Bottom: Two color movie posters depicting the 1940's screen Holmes, Basil Rathbone. In *Sherlock Holmes in Washington*, Rathbone appears as Holmes, and Nigel Bruce is cast as a rather elderly Dr. Watson. The pair find themselves in Washington, helping to save the United States from Nazi spies. The Voice of Terror poster shows that the allure of women is starting to feature in the marketing of Holmes.

Above: Peter Cushing starred as Holmes in the 1959 remake of *The Hound of the Baskervilles,* alongside Andre Morell as Dr. Watson.

Holmes movie, *Sherlock Holmes and the Deadly Necklace* (1962). His gaunt and brooding Sherlock was compelling. Born in 1922, Lee was a graduate of Rank Studio's Charm School, and was particularly famous for his role as Dracula in several Hammer horror movies. He later revived his part in the Holmes "franchise," playing Watson in *Sherlock Holmes and the Leading*

Lady (1990), and *The Incident at Victoria Falls* (1991). He was also cast as a much-too-thin Mycroft Holmes in the 1970 movie, *The Private Life of Sherlock Holmes*.

But Lee was not the only Holmes of the '60s. John Neville took the role in 1965's *A Study in Terror*. As well as being the second color Holmes movie, *Terror* was also the first film to show Holmes tackling Jack the Ripper, in highly apocryphal style.

Above: Christopher Plummer as Holmes in the 1978 film *Murder By Decree.*

A plethora of actors took the big screen role of Holmes in the 1970s, with varying degrees of success. Robert Stephens plays the character in Billy Wilder's highly acclaimed 1970 movie, *The Private Life of Sherlock Holmes*. George C. Scott was also reasonably successful in the movie version of the Broadway play *They Might be Giants* in 1971. Nicol Williamson's performance as Sherlock was also perfectly respectable in 1975's *Seven Percent Solution*, but Roger Moore's 1976 appearance as the great detective in *Sherlock Holmes in New York* confirms that he is a much more successful 007.

Two very different actors played the role of the (adult) Holmes in the 1980s, Michael Caine and Sir Ian Richardson. Caine plays an actor playing Holmes in the fairly successful comedy of 1988, *Without a Clue*, with Ben Kingsley very well cast as Watson. By contrast, classically trained Shakespearian Ian Richardson takes a rather more serious stab at the role in the 1983 films *The Sign of Four* and *The Hound of the Baskervilles*. Interestingly, Richardson was to reappear in a Holmesian setting as Dr. Joseph Bell in 2000's successful television series, *The Murder Rooms*.

Director Steven Spielberg also launched a completely different take on the Holmes character in 1985; with his film *Young Sherlock Holmes*, starring Nicholas Row. As the tagline ran, "Before a Lifetime of Adventure, they had the Adventure of a Lifetime." The film was spun-off into a television series.

But by far the most important contribution to the role of Holmes for this decade (and some would argue to date) was seen on the small screen, rather than at the movies, when Jeremy Brett (1933 to 1995) was cast as Sherlock in the Granada Television series. He went on to star in thirty-six stories and four feature-length television movies, playing against two excellent Watsons: David Burke until 1985, and the superlative Edward Hardwicke for the balance of the work. Brett's florid and melodramatic Sherlock evoked very strong reactions, both positive and negative, but many consider his interpretation to be the ultimate Holmes. Dame Jean Conan Doyle described him as "The Holmes of my youth." Brett was an Eton-educated English actor who had done a stint in Hollywood, appearing in *My Fair Lady*. As well as utterly contradicting some of the dreary early interpretations of Holmes, he was also able to bring his great intelligence to the role, to make Holmes interesting and relevant to modern audiences. Brett also left us an incisive estimation of Holmes's personality: "He is complex. He loves music — he plays the violin very well — he enjoys a joke, he is vain, maybe a little conceited. He likes to be

Above: The late Jeremy Brett as Granada Television's enigmatic Holmes.

Above right: Brett with David Burke as Watson. Burke left the series after thirteen episodes. His portrayal of Watson is judged to be one of the closest to the original Conan Doyle character. Edward Hardwicke succeeded him in the role.

praised. He can be bitchy when he assesses other great detectives. On a difficult case he may build up a considerable tension within himself, which explodes in a genial bit of theatricality when the problem is solved." It was Brett's ambition to film the entire canon, but ill health intervened, and this was never realized.

The 1990s and early 2000s saw a surprising dearth of big screen Sherlock movies. In 1985, seasoned film actor Edward Woodward starred as Holmes in a made-for-television film, *The Hands of A Murderer*, and this trend has continued. A Canadian production of *The Hound of the Baskervilles* was made for television in 2000, starring Matthew Frewer. The film boasted the dubious tagline, "Every Dog has its Day." The BBC made a more serious adaptation of the book in 2002, starring Richard Roxburgh as Sherlock, and Ian Hart as an unusually sharp-witted and complex Watson. The BBC version was surprisingly successful, with a genuinely suspenseful and authentic atmosphere. It is probably the latest version of one of the most-filmed books of all time.

As well as relatively conventional adaptations of the Canon, there have also been some extraordinarily strange interpretations of Conan Doyle's stories. In the 1970s, several strange anomalies reached the small screen. These included Larry Hagman in the truly bizarre television pilot, *The Return of the World's Greatest Detective*. Playing an L.A. motorcycle cop who has a fall, and wakes up believing he is Sherlock Holmes, Hagman gives a very unusual performance. Unsurprisingly, the series was never made. In

1977, the BBC made a much more successful parody of *The Hound of the Baskervilles,* starring comedians Peter Cooke and Dudley Moore. As well as taking the part of Watson, Dudley Moore also makes a cameo appearance as Holmes's mother. Rival British television channel ITV also launched a Holmes comedy, *The Strange Case of the End of Civilisation as We Know It,* starring Monty Python comedian John Cleese: this version bombed.

Of course, Conan Doyle himself left a legacy of Sherlockian stage plays, including the often-revived *Speckled Band* of 1910. Gillette's play has also undergone numerous revivals over the years. Although many of these stage reincarnations of Holmes have been critically successful, the casting for some has been rather peculiar. Charlton Heston, for example, appeared as Holmes in a new stage play *Crucifer of Blood* in 1991, with Jeremy Brett as cast as Watson.

But Conan Doyle's characters have also appeared in far more uncharted territory. The musical *Holmes!* received its first public performance in 1997. As well as the inevitable singing, the great detective finally finds love in this version. 1953 also saw a rather surreal incarnation of Holmes, in a ballet. *The Great Detective* was performed by the Sadler's Wells Company, with Kenneth Macmillan taking the lead role.

As well as being intrinsic to popular English-language culture, Holmes has also appeared in many foreign-language dramatizations. French actor Georges Treville made twelve Holmes films for the French Éclair film company in 1912, while German actor Bruno Guttner appeared as Sherlock in a Nazi-filmed version of the *Hound of the Baskervilles* (1938). Radovan Lukavsky appeared as a big screen Czech Holmes in 1971.

But perhaps the most famous "foreign" Holmes ever is the Russian actor, Vasili Livanov. Livanov appeared on Russian television in several Holmesian dramas in the late 1970s and 1980s, and his representation of the great detective is said to have been a favorite of both the Queen and Margaret Thatcher. He has even been awarded an OBE for his Sherlockian achievement.

It is worth remembering that even apocryphal Holmesian "entertainments" owe their existence to Conan Doyle's characters, and the fascination that they continue to exert. It is extraordinary that the literary ensemble he created back in the 1880s remains so instantly recognizable. Incredible, too, that Conan Doyle's undisputed contribution to so many cultural forms is enjoyed by millions who will never open one of his published works.

Below: Russian actor Vasili Livanov was a favorite of the Queen in his characterization of Holmes for Russian television.

The Canon in Alphabetical order, with its Classic Abbreviations

Early Sherlockian Jay Finley Christ devised the familiar four-letter abbreviation for all sixty works of the Sherlock Holmes Canon. Finley Christ was the author of several important Holmesian works, including An Irregular Guide to Sherlock Holmes of Baker Street (1947), and The Fiction of Sir Arthur Conan Doyle (1959).

The Adventure of the Abbey Grange	ABBE
The Adventure of the Beryl Coronet	BERY
The Adventure of Peter Black	BLAC
The Adventure of the Blanched Soldier	BLAN
The Adventure of the Blue Carbuncle	BLUE
The Boscombe Valley Mystery	BOSC
The Adventure of the Bruce-Partington Plans	BRUC
The Adventure of the Cardboard Box	CARD
The Adventure of Charles Augustus Milverton	CHAS
The Adventure of the Copper Beeches	COPP
The Adventure of the Creeping Man	CREE
The Adventure of the Crooked Man	CROO
The Adventure of the Dancing Men	DANC
The Adventure of the Devil's Foot	DEVI
The Adventure of the Dying Detective	DYIN
The Adventure of the Empty House	EMPT
The Adventure of the Engineer's Thumb	ENGR
The Adventure of the Final Problem	FINA
The Adventure of the Five Orange Pips	FIVE
The Adventure of the Gloria Scott	GLOR
The Adventure of the Golden Pince-nez	GOLD
The Greek Interpreter	GREE
The Hound of the Baskervilles	HOUN
A Case of Identity	IDEN
The Adventure of the Illustrious Client	ILLU
The Disappearance of Lady Frances Carfax	LADY
His Last Bow	LAST
The Adventure of the Lion's Mane	LION
The Adventure of the Mazarin Stone	MAZA
The Adventure of the Missing Three-Quarter	MISS
The Adventure of the Musgrave Ritual	MUSG
The Naval Treaty	NAVA
The Adventure of the Noble Bachelor	NOBL
The Adventure of the Norwood Builder	NORW
The Adventure of the Priory School	PRIO
The Adventure of the Red Circle	REDC
The Red-Headed League	REDH
The Reigate Squires	REIG
The Resident Patient	RESI
The Adventure of the Retired Colourman	RETI
A Scandal in Bohemia	SCAN
The Adventure of the Second Stain	SECO
The Adventure of Shoscombe Old Place	SHOS
The Sign of the Four	SIGN
Silver Blaze	SILV
The Adventure of the Six Napoleons	SIXN
The Adventure of the Solitary Cyclist	SOLI
The Adventure of the Speckled Band	SPEC
The Stockbroker's Clerk	STOC
A Study in Scarlet	STUD
The Adventure of the Sussex Vampire	SUSS
The Problem of Thor Bridge	THOR
The Adventure of the Three Gables	3GAB
The Adventure of the Three Garridebs	3GAR
The Adventure of the Three Students	3STU
The Man with the Twisted Lip	TWIS
The Valley of Fear	VALL
The Adventure of the Veiled Lodger	VEIL
The Adventure of Wisteria Lodge	WIST
The Yellow Face	YELL

Arthur Conan Doyle's Ten Favorite Canon Stories
Over the years, several famous lists of favorite Sherlock Holmes stories have been published. Arthur Conan Doyle published his list of his twelve stories in 1927 in the Strand.
1. The Adventure of the Speckled Band
2. The Red-Headed League
3. The Adventure of the Dancing Men
4. The Adventure of the Final Problem
5. A Scandal in Bohemia
6. The Adventure of the Empty House
7. The Five Orange Pips
8. The Adventure of the Second Stain
9. The Adventure of the Devil's Foot
10. The Adventure of the Priory School
11. The Adventure of the Musgrave Ritual
12. The Adventure of the Reigate Squires

In 1959, the in-house magazine of the Baker Street Irregulars, The Baker Street Journal, published their list of ten favorite Canon stories.
1. The Adventure of the Speckled Band
2. The Red-Headed League
3. The Adventure of the Blue Carbuncle
4. The Adventure of Silver Blaze
5. A Scandal in Bohemia
6. The Adventure of the Musgrave Ritual
7. The Adventure of the Bruce-Partington Plans
8. The Adventure of the Six Napoleons
9. The Adventure of the Dancing Men
10. The Adventure of the Empty House

Acknowledgments

John Aidiniantz, Assistant Curator, The Sherlock Holmes Museum, 221B Baker Street, London (www.sherlock-holmes.co.uk)
The British Film Institute
Brian W. Pugh, Curator of the Conan Doyle (Crowborough) Establishment
John Endicott, Curator, The Kent Police Museum (www.Kent-police-museum.co.uk)
Christie's, London
Mister Antony Inverness Capes (www.misterantony.com)
The Royal Commission on the Ancient & Historical Monuments of Scotland
Bjarne Nielsen, Sherlock Holmes Museet, Denmark
Michael J.T. Lee, The Traditional Games Company Ltd.
Troy Taylor, The American Ghost Society
University of California San Francisco, School of Medicine